RIDING HIGH

They sat together, talking easily, until the position of the sun in the west told Jessica that she had to get back to Holly Hills.

She turned to climb into the saddle, but Simon put his hand on her shoulder, stopping her.

"Jessica," he murmured softly.

And then she was in his arms, and he was kissing her hard, holding her against him. Her arm tightened around his neck and her eyes closed as she gave herself up to his kiss. It was like no other kiss she had ever received.

She was in love. She couldn't wait to tell the other Jessicas . . . but what was it about this handsome horseman that seemed too good to be true . . . ?

HEARTS & DIAMONDS # 2

THE FOUR JESSICAS

by

Leonore Fleischer

A SIGNET VISTA BOOK
NEW AMERICAN LIBRARY

NAL BOOKS ARE AVAILABLE AT QUANTITY DISCOUNTS WHEN USED TO PROMOTE PRODUCTS OR SERVICES. FOR INFORMATION PLEASE WRITE TO PREMIUM MARKETING DIVISION, NEW AMERICAN LIBRARY, 1633 BROADWAY, NEW YORK, NEW YORK 10019.

RL6/IL8+

SIGNET VISTA TRADEMARK REG. U.S. PAT. OFF. AND FOREIGN COUNTRIES
REGISTERED TRADEMARK—MARCA REGISTRADA
HECHO EN CHICAGO, IL., U.S.A.

SIGNET, SIGNET CLASSIC, MENTOR, PLUME, MERIDIAN and NAL BOOKS
are published by New American Library,
1633 Broadway, New York, New York 10019

First Printing, March, 1986

1 2 3 4 5 6 7 8 9

PRINTED IN THE UNITED STATES OF AMERICA

Dedicated to
one Jessica, Jessica Fleischer;
one Jennifer, Jennifer Livingston;
and one Douglas, Douglas Newell Mount.

HOLLY HILLS

♥

When Holly Hills was founded, back in 1830, as a private boarding school for young ladies of good family, it was years ahead of its time. Although its students learned all the accomplishments expected of Victorian girls—music, painting on fans and china, fine needlework and Bible—also emphasized was the importance of the mind. Included in the Holly Hills curriculum were mathematics, geography, history, Latin, Greek, French, German, the less bawdy of the English poets, and fine penmanship, which today might be called "penpersonship."

The twentieth century has caught up with Holly Hills. The girls now elect to take computer science, feminist literature, short story writing, modern dance and classical ballet, pottery, theater, driver education, modern marriage, and archeology, as well as the usual science and humanities courses. A liberal scholarship program has brought girls from every economic walk of life to Holly Hills. But one thing hasn't changed. To be known as a Holly Hills girl you have to be smart and work hard. As a reward, the Holly Hills graduate is gladly accepted by every good university and college in America.

Holly Hills is a girls' school, true, but it's surrounded by boys' schools, the nearest one, Chatham, being only six miles away. Tucked into the rolling Connecticut countryside, surrounded by bushes of evergreen, Holly Hills offers crisp autumns and tender springs, deep white winters with sleigh rides and skating parties, and many opportunities for falling in love. Especially for falling in love . . .

CHAPTER ONE

Two Jessicas

It's not every girl who could become a legend in a school like Holly Hills, especially in her own lifetime, but one year four girls made it. Much of the mythology that the other students wove around them was made up of nostalgia, exaggeration, envy, and wishful thinking. If the rest of the sophs had known the *whole* story, the legend would have been at least twice as vivid.

The first of the two Jessicas were Jessica Marshall and Jessica Brown. At first sight they were an unlikely pair assigned to be lab partners in Ms. Fenwick's freshman biology class.

"I hope you're going to be serious about this," Jessica Brown told Jessica Marshall with some skepticism on their first day in the laboratory. "I'm going to be a microbiologist, so a good grade in this course is important to me."

Jessica Marshall tossed back her pale, soft hair—her bangs were always threatening to flop over her eyes—and answered indignantly, "What makes you presume that this course isn't important to *me*? For your information, I'm going to study veterinary medicine, so I'll be holding up *my* end, thank you!"

The two girls glared at each other. The taller of them, Jessica Brown, was five feet eight and still growing. Although her features were plain, her eyes were extraordinary, a deep rare gray outlined by extra-long, extra-thick lashes a few shades darker than her glossy black hair. Jessica Brown wore her hair pulled away from her face and braided tightly, the braid hanging down her back almost to her waist.

Jessica Marshall was a genuine beauty and her incredible looks triggered Jessica Brown's suspicions. She found it hard to picture this sun-warmed, blue-eyed blonde with the blossoming figure and the delicate hands doing anything as down-to-earth as giving distemper shots to cats and dogs or treating cows for hoof-and-mouth disease. Jessica Brown was convinced there could be nothing resembling a brain in that golden fluff of Jessica Marshall's head.

But, since they had no choice in being assigned to each other, the two of them struck an uneasy truce and set to work.

It soon became apparent to Jessica Brown that her suspicions were unfounded. Jessica Marshall was not only a hard worker, she was brilliant, almost as brilliant as Jessica Brown herself. As a plus, she could produce miraculous drawings, meticulous and accurate, illustrating cell division, the inner structure of the maple leaf, almost any biological topic in all its natural glory. Jessica Brown's strength lay in correlating the data derived from the experiments and wording the conclusions, so the papers the two Jessicas turned in to Miss Fenwick were minor masterpieces, and were graded accordingly.

Soon Jessica Marshall and Jessica Brown became a team outside the biology lab as well. Anyone observing them would remark that they were an unlikely duo. Brown was from New England, the rugged coast of Maine, and was, like the granite on which the coast is built, strong, plain, and sensible. She wore sturdy shoes, a pleated tartan skirt, and Shetland sweaters knitted to last forever. She called her jeans "dungarees" and never wore them to class. They were baggy and swam around on her thin body, doing absolutely nothing for her.

Jessica Marshall had grown up in Wyoming, where her parents owned—or rather shared in the hard work of—a small horse farm. She had spent most of her leisure hours on the back of her palomino pony, Moonlight Sonata, and her hair was almost the exact color of the pony's mane, a rich, pale gold. Bubbly, with a strong sense of fun, she was the perfect foil for the sober Jessica Brown. And Jessica Marshall *lived* in her jeans, which were worn, faded, and very tight.

There was nothing unusual about two girls having the same first name, especially when the name was so popular. After all, fifteen years ago, half the freshman class had been named Linda, and only ten years past most of the class was called Lisa. But when the two Jessicas were joined at the beginning of sophomore year by Jessica Prud'homme de la Reaux, the group started to attract some attention at Holly Hills. And when, three weeks into the semester, Jessica Rudolph came to the school, the little group of girls began to be known as "the four Jessicas." It was the stuff of which legends are made.

Jessica Rudolph sparked them and gave the group its character and style. She was the catalyst, unifying them in a tight and self-sufficient clique. When the big trouble came, it was Jessica Rudolph who'd help them find the strength to come through it as a group. But before anybody ever even dreamed of Jessica Rudolph, Jessica Prud' homme de la Reaux made her entrance into Holly Hills.

As an elite private school, Holly Hills had seen its share of astonishing arrivals. Up to now, nobody had descended on its green lawns in a hot-air balloon or emerged from its skating pond in a submarine, but that's about it. Once there had been a police squad car for a district attorney's daughter and a stretch Cadillac with diplomatic plates for a fifteen-year-old princess from West Africa. Even so, most of the girls arrived merely by train or by station wagon, accompanied by one or more parents. Amanda Cohen turned up at school the first time trailing *four* parents in her wake: Mother and Father, Mother's New Husband, and Father's New Wife. Such was the power of Amanda Cohen.

But Jessica Prud'homme de la Reaux arrived at Holly Hills a full day after term had started, by motorcade.

In the lead roared a double motorcycle escort flanking her limo. Between the two powerful bikes purred the diplomatic limousine itself, a Daimler-Benz, complete with armor plating, one-way glass and flags flying from the hood of the car. A station wagon piled high with Jessica's luggage followed the limo at a humble and discreet distance.

Classes were already in session, but the shrieking of the motorcycle sirens drew everybody to the windows, even the teachers. Miss Appleyard, the august mistress of Holly Hills, resplendent in a Ballantyne cashmere sweater set, a perfectly pleated gray skirt, well-shined brogans from Bally of Switzerland, and a string of real pearls around her patrician throat, appeared at the front door herself. Everyone knew that whoever was inside that limo must be one important student if The Apple was waiting for her on the doorstep!

The Daimler-Benz braked to a stop on the driveway. The doors of the limo opened, and two men in black suits leaped out and flanked the automobile. No one at Holly Hills had ever laid eyes on a real live bodyguard before, and it created a sensation of epic proportions!

Meanwhile, servants had begun to drag out large trunks and hampers from the station wagon. This was no ordinary Holly Hills girl, this could be no less than Cleopatra of Egypt!

But where was the new girl? Who was the owner of all those exciting and very expensive suitcases and trunks? Whose importance commanded a couple of armed guards?

"Madame, may I introduce to you Mademoiselle Jessica Prud'homme de la Reaux?" The tall gentleman with the girl bowed slightly. The girl flinched.

She was no bigger than a cricket! A tiny girl with huge, timid eyes, Jessica Prud'homme de la Reaux was dressed in the height of expensive fashion, *haute couture* down to the thin little Maud Frizon sandals on her narrow feet. She looked lost inside those clothes, as though her outfit was wearing her instead of the other way around. Maybe she was filthy rich, with clothes to kill for, but the girl was a loser, that much was evident. Immediately, the girls at the window lost interest.

"I'm happy to meet you, my child." The Apple offered a welcoming smile. The girl smiled back timidly, and the headmistress took a step forward, placing a gentle arm around Jessica's thin shoulders.

"And you are her father?"

"Mais non, madame," said the tall man. "His Excellency the ambassador has urgent business in Washington today. I am merely his aide, Eugène Leroi. I've accompanied Mademoiselle Jessica to see her settle in comfortably . . . and safely." Eugène Leroi glanced significantly at the two bodyguards, who were standing at attention, their eyes moving quickly and constantly around the quadrangle, checking for . . . what?

"Then we thank you very much," said Miss Appleyard briskly, drawing the girl toward the front door. "But we can take care of her now. She will be . . . safe . . . with us." Her voice touched on the word with some disdain.

"Madame, I beg your pardon, but I have been instructed very firmly by the ambassador . . ." The aide waved in the direction of the bodyguards. "They must remain—"

"Impossible!" barked the Apple. "I forbid you to leave those men behind. Holly Hills will take full responsibility for this student, as we do for *all* our girls. Do you think this is the only diplomat's daughter we have enrolled here? Why, we've had *princesses* who were Holly Hills girls, and no harm came to them!"

"But this case is different." The aide lowered his voice.

Jessica Prud'homme de la Reaux was trembling harder than ever, and her huge begging eyes followed Miss Appleyard like a whipped puppy's.

"No wonder this child is frightened half to death!" cried the headmistress. "I would be, too, with those thugs around, and threats flying over my head." The girls who were listening shook their heads doubtfully; the Apple could never be afraid of *anything*.

It was a standoff, with neither side willing to budge an inch. At last Miss Appleyard put a call into the embassy in Washington. When the motorcade left Holly Hills, sirens screaming, the two bodyguards left with it.

Well! The girls giggled, nudging each other with pleasure. *Wasn't that something else?* It was better than a Clint Eastwood movie.

In the next three weeks, it was evident that poor little Jessica Prud'homme de la Reaux was not going to get any happier than she'd been when she'd arrived. She had been assigned a dormitory room all to herself, a tiny one close by the dorm mistress's room (as though fussy little Mrs. Hayward could foil any serious attempts on the part of kidnappers). Only a small percentage of her extensive, expensive wardrobe, much of it more suitable for dancing at the Starlight Roof than to classes at a New England girls' school, had been unpacked and jammed tightly into the single closet and small bureau. The rest was crammed in the trunks that took up the rest of the space in her room.

Unpacking had been the highlight of her stay so far. The girls in the dorm had crowded into Jessica's room and hung around the doorway to watch the Paris labels and the *Vogue* model outfits being unfolded from the tissue paper. Little Amanda Cohen, who had a lifetime subscription to *Women's Wear Daily* and lived to shop, took a front-row seat on the floor and kept up a running commentary as each garment was shaken out and jammed into the closet by a nervous Jessica Prud'homme de la Reaux.

"That's a real Oscar, girls. Oscar de la Renta. The *copies* of that one cost a thousand bucks! What have we here? It's to die! Kenzo! The cape *and* the tunic; have you got the matching boots, Jessica? Yup, here come the boots. Girls, we couldn't even afford the *leg warmers* that go with that outfit."

When the closet and the dresser held all that they could hold, the girls got up and left, including Amanda, who asked to borrow the Kenzo. Jessica Prud'homme de la Reaux sat alone on her bed, feeling abandoned and miserable.

She went to her classes unobtrusively and without too much difficulty, although she was too shy to recite when called on. Her education thus far had been superb; her French was flawless, her grasp of history and literature mature and thoughtful, and even mathematics, her one real area of weakness, was less frightening here than it had been at her last school.

But Jessica Prud'homme de la Reaux seemed unable to enjoy or even participate in any of the wonderful things for which Holly Hills was famous. She didn't try out for sports, join extracurricular clubs, audition for theater or dance, or attend any of the mixers that brought the surrounding boys' schools down for an evening of chaperoned dancing. All around her, Holly Hills girls were making friends who would last through the school years and often even through life. But Jessica Prud'homme de la Reaux had no friends. She was too timid to make any overtures herself, and the other girls stayed away from her.

Some of them thought she was stuck up because she was so rich and her father so famous. Others had taken seriously the vague rumors of "kidnap" and "terrorists" and didn't want to be too close by when the school was stormed by the Red Guard or the Shiite Muslims. Still others, like Jessica Marshall and Jessica Brown, had already formed their friendships in their freshman year and simply weren't interested or didn't have the time to extend their circle.

As freshmen, the girls were assigned four to a room; in their sophomore year, only two girls shared a room, and they could choose their own roomies. Jessica Marshall and Jessica Brown had chosen each other, and both were satisfied with the arrangement. They studied well together and even double-dated from time to time, whenever beautiful Jessica Marshall could persuade the boy who was in love with her at the moment to bring along a date for her plainer roomie.

Love didn't mean too much to Jessica Brown; whenever she said the word *love,* and her face softened, her roommate knew she was thinking of her golden retriever, Brandy. Having grown up as the only daughter in a big family, surrounded by five brothers, three older and two younger, Jessica Brown was not romantic about boys. She had few illusions. She knew she would probably marry, but all that was long into the future and hardly worth thinking about now.

Sometimes Jessica Marshall realized ruefully that *she* thought about little else besides boys. Besides being beautiful, she was a born romantic, and wept buckets over Jane Austen's novels, especially the happy endings.

"My lord," snorted Jessica Brown scornfully, "you even cry during Mountain Dew TV commercials."

"I can't help it," confessed Jessica Marshall. "They're so *beautiful*! And the boys are so handsome!"

An only child, Jessica Marshall thought boys were miraculous, beautiful strong beings with exciting interests. Ever since the first mixer in her freshman year, she had fallen in love regularly, at two-month intervals. Because she was so very pretty, so exuberant and enthusiastic, boys almost always fell in love with her in return. The phone was always for her; her Saturday nights were usually spoken for weeks in advance; and on Sunday morning, she would tell Jessica Brown all the details—what he said, how he looked, whether or not they'd danced; whether or not she'd let him kiss her. The details were almost always the same; it was the boys' names that kept changing. Jessica Brown often lost track of her lovely roommate's social life, and was sometimes behind by as much as two boys at a time.

"How's that . . . whatshisname . . . Peter?"

"Honestly, Jessica! I haven't seen *him* in *months*!"

"Well, how am I supposed to keep up?"

Yet with all the popularity she enjoyed, and all the fun she had on dates, Jessica Marshall knew that she had not yet found *true* love, and it was true love of which she dreamed.

CHAPTER TWO

Three Jessicas

A summons to Miss Appleyard's office held all the solemnity and terror of the funeral procession of a king. Jessica Marshall and Jessica Brown had been summoned, and approached the inner sanctum nervously. But the headmistress greeted them both with a warm smile and outstretched hands.

"Come in, girls. I'm happy to see you. Please take seats."

Puzzled, they sat.

Miss Appleyard's face became more serious. "Girls, I'm going to ask you to do Holly Hills and me a real favor."

Now the two Jessicas were mystified. They allowed the Apple to continue.

"I know you two are good friends, and I know that what I'm asking you to do won't be easy, but I would like one of you to room with Jessica Prud'homme de la Reaux." At their gasp, the Apple held up an aristocratic hand.

"Hear me out. I've given this a lot of thought. I need a girl who is mature, a girl who is a good student, an honorable person, and somebody self-sufficient enough to be able to take this poor child on and befriend her. It's important that she be helped by one of her peer group, not a member of the faculty. I think your friendship will withstand this—I hesitate to call it an intrusion, but I suppose that's what it is. . . ."

Jessica Brown cleared her throat. "Miss Appleyard, do

we understand that you want to break us up and stick Jessica Pudding de la Whatsherface in with one of us?" She was so incensed that she totally forgot to whom she was speaking.

Fortunately, at the moment the Apple was in no position to call her on her manners.

"Well, that's a harsh way to put it, but in effect, yes."

"Which one of us?"

The headmistress's smooth brow creased in a frown. "That's the most difficult part. Either one of you would be perfect. But I would choose the girl who could honestly tell me that she wouldn't resent Jessica Prud'homme de la Reaux because of it, that she'd be the best possible friend she knew how to be, a real Holly Hills girl."

Jessica Marshall looked at Jessica Brown. Jessica Brown looked back at Jessica Marshall. A minute of silence ensued, while both girls thought it over.

Then Jessica Marshall took a deep breath. "Miss Appleyard, may . . . may I make an alternate suggestion?"

Miss Appleyard raised her patrician eyebrow and nodded.

"Well, instead of breaking the two of us up, what if you put Jessica Prud'homme de la Reaux in the room with *both* of us? We really would look after her, and I promise we'd include her and help her the best way we can. That way, she'd have *two* friends instead of one. And we wouldn't have to resent her."

Miss Appleyard looked at Jessica Brown, who was nodding in doubtful agreement. The Apple's fingers tapped her desk as she thought it over.

"Very well, then, it's settled," she said at last. "I'm very pleased with you, girls. I'm pleased with both of you. You've handled this situation like true Holly Hills students. I'm sure that Jessica Prud'homme de la Reaux will benefit greatly by this association. And who knows?

You may find benefit in it yourselves." She laughed. "Why, now you'll be three Jessicas all together. That hadn't occurred to me before."

When Miss Appleyard's door had closed behind them, Jessica Brown turned to Jessica Marshall. "Now what?" she asked gloomily.

"Now I guess we're stuck baby-sitting."

"For the rest of the school year."

Jessica Marshall shook her pretty head. "Don't forget, we'll be 'three Jessicas all together.' ''

"Terrific. That's exactly what we needed. Another Jessica. And where do you suppose we'll be able to store that mountain of designer threads she trucked in with her? And what are you going to do with her on your precious date nights? Drag her along with her teddy bear or stick me with her? Do I get to sing her a lullaby and rock her to sleep?" Jessica Brown's voice dripped with hurt sarcasm.

Jessica Marshall sighed. "I hadn't thought of any of that," she admitted remorsefully.

"That's the trouble with you! You *don't* think! Now look at us," said Jessica Brown in despair. "She hasn't even moved in yet, and we're fighting already."

"Look, I promise to hold up my end. I'll spend as much time with her as you will. After all, what was the alternative? The Apple was about to break the two of us up. Would you have liked that better?"

"Of course not! It's just that . . . well, I wish you'd consulted me first before shooting your mouth off to the Apple. We could have asked for an hour to think it over and maybe come up with a plan."

"What plan?" demanded Jessica Marshall.

"How should I know? You never even gave me a chance to think! And now we're stuck with her. Rich, pampered, snooty, wimpy, and all ours! The three Jessicas, yuck!

That's so cutesy I could barf!'' And Jessica Brown turned angrily on her heel and stalked off.

Three days later, a bed and dresser were jammed into the two Jessicas' bedroom, followed by the famous wardrobe trunks and little Jessica Prud'homme de la Reaux herself, anxiety written all over her tiny features.

She barely spoke a word to the other two, aware that she was intruding upon a close friendship, that she was the outsider. But it wasn't snobbery she was displaying, although that's the way her new roommates took it at first, before they came to know her better. It was real and painful shyness.

How could it possibly be easy, with the three of them crammed into a room meant for two? After Jessica Brown had barked her shins for the sixth time in two days on the sharp corner of the Louis Vuitton wardrobe trunk, she really lost her temper. Jessica Prud'homme de la Reaux packed away most of her expensive clothing and shipped it back to the embassy in Washington. Most of it was unsuitable for school anyway. She kept one large suitcase stowed under her bed.

Then there was the matter of their names. Miss Appleyard might have thought it quaint, but it was really a logistical pain. Jessica Brown and Jessica Marshall were accustomed to calling each other ''Jessica.'' When there were only two girls in a room, there wasn't much doubt about who was speaking to whom. But with three . . . They tried calling one another by last names, but ''Marshall'' and ''Brown'' sounded awkward to them, and ''Prud'homme de la Reaux'' was not only ridiculous but unpronounceable. They tried ''Jessica One,'' ''Jessica Two,'' and ''Jessica Three,'' but that was no better, even though Jessica Prud'homme de la Reaux instantly agreed to be "Three." So they began to resign themselves to asking "Me?" whenever the three of them were together and somebody said "Jessica."

There seemed to be some doubt as to whether they were doing Jessica Prud'homme de la Reaux any good. She continued to have very little to say for herself, although Jessica Marshall was genuinely curious about life in the diplomatic service and asked her many questions in an attempt to draw her out.

It seemed the poor girl had rarely seen the outside of her room. She'd been brought up by governesses and had at first been educated by special tutors at home. In the past few years, she had been allowed to go to school and had attended famous and expensive schools in Switzerland and France, but Europe, it seemed, was not "safe." Too many kidnappings, too many terrorist incidents. Her father the ambassador, checking around, had hit upon Holly Hills, and to Holly Hills his only child had been sent. As to her own preference, nobody had ever asked her about it.

Every single day, punctually at five o'clock in the evening, Jessica Prud'homme de la Reaux received a long-distance telephone call. She would be on the line for about ten minutes, giving a blow-by-blow account of every event of her uneventful day. Which classes she had attended, whether or not she had recited and, if she had, how her answers had been received. Exactly what she'd eaten, what she'd worn, who she'd been spending her time with. It was a pitiful little dry accounting, never once lightened by amusing or joyous anecdotes. Of her sorrow and loneliness she said not a word.

Her roommates at first believed that it was her father on the other end of the telephone until they learned by chance that it was only her father's aide-de-camp, who would then report the conversation back to the ambassador. Jessica

Prud'homme de la Reaux never even got to tell her own father how she was doing.

"She's the loneliest person I've ever met," said Jessica Marshall sadly. "I mean, I grew up on a ranch, where we were snowed in for weeks every winter, but I can't ever remember being *that* lonely. Not with Mom and Dad and the horses around. And the cat was always having kittens."

Jessica Brown shook her head. "With five brothers, I sometimes *prayed* to be all alone by myself. But now that I see it . . . brrr. You can have it!"

"What can we do? She doesn't want to come to glee club or dramatics. She won't go riding with me or play tennis with you. Our biggest breakthrough was that chess game, but she didn't utter a single word except 'check' and 'checkmate.' She destroyed me in eight moves and went right back to her book."

"We can only try." Jessica Brown sighed. "We did promise to be Holly Hill girls. But she creeps around like a mouse and I swear to you it's getting on my nerves! I don't know how much longer I can take her whispering and her tiptoeing. Sometimes I want to tie a bell around her neck so I can hear her coming. The other day she snuck up behind me and I almost jumped out of my skin. Can't we put taps on her shoes?"

"It's not the creeping around I mind as much as the crying in bed at night when she thinks we're asleep. I have to admit that really gets to me. I don't know what to do—hug her or strangle her!"

Standing unseen outside the doorway, hearing every word, Jessica Prud'homme de la Reaux crept away in tears. She knew that she was putting a strain on her roommates' friendship, on the patience of everybody around her, but she was already so unhappy that it almost didn't matter. It seemed to her that, small as she was, there was no room in the world for her. Everybody had a place, everybody had a friend. Everybody but her.

This was the heavy situation three weeks into the term when the rumor flew around the school like a lightning bolt that Jessica Rudolph would be coming to Holly Hills. But it was excitement tinged with sympathy.

Jessica Rudolph, winner of the Junior Division gymnastics championship, had been the most promising young gymnast to emerge in America in the past decade. Her floor work was brilliantly artistic and her movements on the horse and the parallel bars were unequaled in her division. Teenage girls all over America idolized her and identified with her. *Sports Illustrated* put her on its cover and said she was America's best hope to defeat the Czechs, Rumanians, and Russians at the next Olympics. Everybody was counting on Jessica Rudolph to bring home the gold.

But Jessica Rudolph didn't bring home the gold. After winning the divisional, she fell from the balance beam and injured her knee badly. It was only a practice session, but it cost her the next Olympics and any hope of a gold medal. Two operations later, it was still doubtful whether the girl would ever again do an aerial leap on the high bar. She had been a soaring bird, poetry in motion; now she was grounded, flightless, a bird with damaged wings.

Yes, the rumors were true. Yes, Jessica Rudolph was coming to Holly Hills. Yes, she was still on crutches. Yes, they would have to be very careful around her, all of them. The Holly Hills girls, who could still ski, skate, dance, and run would have to watch what they said and did around the fallen gladiator.

They planned to wait outside to greet her arrival, all three hundred girls lining up beside the driveway, as a fitting way to greet a hero. But on the day she was due, it rained. A heavy, gray, sopping, early October downpour. The fallen autumn leaves were slick underfoot; all the crunch had gone out of them. So much for waiting outside.

By lunchtime, Jessica Rudolph had still not put in her appearance. The girls all trooped into the dining room, grumbling. Wet days always made them gloomy, all but the handful of bookworms who like nothing better than to curl up with an apple and a novel while raindrops pelted the roof.

They had finished their tuna salads and canned peaches and were passing their plates up to the head of the table when the girls of Holly Hills became aware that Miss Appleyard was standing in the doorway of the dining room, waiting for silence. Beside her stood a girl of middle height, with curly red hair and a cheerful face. The girl was leaning on a cane. No crutches, just a cane and a bulky cast around the knee. The buzz of voices circled the room. It was her! More correctly, it was she! Jessica Rudolph!

For the first time in the recollection of anybody in the room, the headmistress spoke without formality. "Here she is, girls," she called proudly. "Here's Jessica!"

With one simultaneous impulse, every girl in the school stood up and began to applaud. The applause grew, swelled, filling the old wood-paneled dining hall, reaching the rafters, totally heartfelt and totally spontaneous.

The redheaded girl took a hopping step backward, as though the welcome was too much for her. Then, grasping the doorknob to steady herself, she waved her cane in the air to greet them. "Far out!" she yelled. "Wow, what a way to say hello! You're a ten bunch of guys! Now, this is what I call a school!"

It was soon evident that the last thing you had to do was walk on eggshells around Jessica Rudolph. She was outgoing and cheerful as she hopped from class to class on her cane. Far from thinking of herself as handicapped, she talked openly of a future in which she would be able to play hockey or go skating. The only thing she refused to talk about was gymnastics. She answered any question put to her, but she wouldn't elaborate on her answers.

Jessica seemed to love everything about Holly Hills. It was the first school she had ever attended since she had shown her first athletic aptitude at the age of five. Her father, a well-do-do Arizona real estate broker, immediately engaged the best gymnastics coach available and relentlessly started Jessica on the long, hard road to the Olympics.

Jessica was snatched out of kindergarten and assigned a series of private tutors. The most important people in her life were her trainer and her coach. The emphasis was on practice, balance, nutrition, practice, and more practice. Math, science, history, literature—Jessica Rudolph had crammed them in haphazardly between sessions on the uneven bars. She grew up in training sweats, with the smell of rosin in her nostrils, and her eye on only one thing—the American championship and the international gold medal.

Just as Jessica Rudolph had the gold almost within her grasp, it had been snatched away from her, leaving her with a swollen, throbbing knee embellished with two long scars on it and all the feelings she kept bottled up inside.

Where was she going to sleep? Who would be her lucky roommate? These were the burning questions on everybody's lips. Whoever got Jessica Rudolph would be twice blessed. Not only would her roommate be honored by the friendship of this heroic girl, but she would inherit by right the fallout from the boys!

It seemed that every boy within a radius of fifty miles— and there were six boys' schools within a radius of fifty miles—wanted to meet Jessica Rudolph. They were as excited at St. Trinity's, at Chalfont, at Cumberland, at Choate, and Andover as they were at Holly Hills. Boys from the surrounding schools, even juniors and seniors, were already beginning to telephone and hopefully leave their names and numbers. Hog heaven!

For the moment, though, Jessica Rudolph had to sleep in the infirmary until the cast came off her knee, so the school doctor could keep one eye on her. Despite her bubbling optimism, she tired easily.

After the first flush of excitement, Jessica Brown and Jessica Marshall went back to their customary routine, but Jessica Prud'homme de la Reaux remained in a kind of daze. Never in her life had she met anybody as charismatic as Jessica Rudolph. And Jessica Prud'homme de la Reaux had once curtsied a real queen! The thunderous applause that had greeted the young athlete's arrival hadn't even fazed Jessica Rudolph! It seemed natural to the little shy girl that one should clap for Jessica Rudolph whenever she came into a room.

For the first time Jessica Prud'homme de la Reaux had a flesh-and-blood idol to worship instead of the heroes in the romantic novels that she devoured. It seemed to her that Jessica Rudolph embodied all the characteristics that she herself so lacked—courage, stamina, independence of spirit, optimism, and irrepressibility.

In addition to her wretched shyness, Jessica Prud'homme de la Reaux was plagued by nervous hypochondria, like the frail heroines in early gothic novels who carried smelling salts in their muffs and fainted at loud noises. In the twentieth century, Jessica Prud'homme de la Reaux's weak nerves took the form of sore throats and easily caught colds.

Which is how she wound up in the infirmary, and found herself on speaking terms with her goddess.

"I wish I could get the hang of this French verb," groused Jessica Rudolph in the next bed.

"Which verb is that?" croaked the other Jessica timidly.

" 'To be.' You'd think that would be the easiest one, wouldn't you? Why does it have to take so many darn forms?"

"It has no more forms than English. 'I *am*, you *are*, he *is* . . .' it's not that much different from *'je suis, tu es, vous êtes, il est.'* See?" Jessica Prud'homme de la Reaux was astonished to find herself speaking so easily to anybody, let alone the celebrated and admired Jessica Rudolph.

"You're pretty good at this stuff, aren't you?"

"Well, it was my first language. We spoke French at home."

"You wouldn't have time to help me with it, I suppose? I'm good at math. So if you need any help with that, we might work out a trade."

It was as though the gray rainy heavens had parted and the golden rays of the sun were bathing Jessica Prud'homme de la Reaux in their blessed radiance. Her tiny face lit up with happiness. *"Mais oui,"* she breathed, marveling at the miracle.

And so the odd friendship between Jessica Rudolph and Jessica Prud'homme de la Reaux began with doing their French and algebra assignments together after class in the infirmary. Jessica Marshall and Jessica Brown were stunned. The most sought-after girl in the sophomore class! Look who was friends with her! It almost didn't seem possible.

"I think I'm jealous," said Jessica Brown to Jessica Marshall. "But I'm not sure. After all, she *is* supposed to be *our* roommate, isn't she? Now she's spending all her spare time in the infirmary with Rudolph."

"Yes, but look at it this way. Have you ever seen her so happy? She actually smiled at us yesterday!"

"I know. You're right. But I can't help feeling that somehow we failed her. It was never *our* friendship she wanted."

"You know what I think?" Jessica Marshall asked suddenly. "I think what she needed was to be needed. That's all. Nobody had ever asked her for anything or shown her that she made a difference. Now she does."

"Do you think that Jessica Rudolph will ask her to room together when she gets out of the infirmary?"

"It could turn out that way . . ." Jessica Marshall narrowed her eyes in thought. "I wouldn't be surprised."

But the way it turned out both Jessica Marshall and Jessica Brown were very surprised.

CHAPTER THREE

Four Jessicas

"All four of you? But only freshmen live four to a room! You girls are sophomores!" Mrs. Hayward, the dorm mistress, looked up to heaven for guidance.

"The thing is, Mrs. Hayward, ma'am, is that we don't want to live like freshmen," answered Jessica Rudolph politely. "These three are crowded enough as it is, without me trying to squeeze myself in. And the doctor says I have to have a clear space around my bed in case of bumping into things, you know? So, I was thinking . . . that very big room on the third floor. Nobody is using it."

"That room! But nobody *ever* uses it, dear. That's not a room for students. When we have an assistant dorm mistress, that's where she lives."

"But we haven't got one this year, have we?" Jessica Brown pressed. "And it's only for this year."

"It's big enough for four, easily," Jessica Marshall put in.

"And it has all those windows," added Jessica Prud'homme de la Reaux wistfully, and unexpectedly. She never spoke unless she was spoken to first, especially to one of the teachers. "It's so bright and airy."

Mrs. Hayward looked flustered, but then, Mrs. Hayward *always* looked flustered. "I don't know . . ." she began doubtfully.

"Please!" came a chorus of four voices.

"We'll have to see what Miss Appleyard says."

"The third-floor room!" exclaimed the Apple, her eyebrows shooting up. "That's the only room on that floor. It seems to me that you girls are asking for special privileges here, and you know that's not the Holly Hill way."

Undaunted, Jessica Rudolph spoke up. "It's true," she admitted frankly. "It *is* something of a special privilege, but it's a privilege we'll try to earn. And it's one that you can revoke if you have to, which we hope you won't, of course," she added hastily.

Miss Appleyard looked around the group. She had never seen so hopeful or expentant a look on Jessica Prud'homme de la Reaux's usually depressed little face. That in itself meant a lot. "But what about your knee? All those stairs."

Jessica Rudolph's face broke into a grin. "Good exercise. I need to walk stairs to strengthen the knee. Besides, it's really only once a day down and once a day up, most days."

The Apple sat silent, lost in thought. Although she didn't approve of granting special privileges—especially those which hadn't been earned yet—she could see some merit in the suggestions. The girls of Holly Hills were always encouraged to develop independence, within bounds, of course. And as Jessica Rudolph had pointed out, the privilege could always be revoked. But would these girls be responsible? Miss Appleyard sighed; it was a difficult decision.

"All right, we'll try it out for a while and see how it goes," said the Apple at last, giving in. "But how are you going to manage? All those Jessicas! You'll be 'the four Jessicas.' " She laughed, more prophetic than she knew.

"Don't worry ma'am, we'll manage. Won't we, Jessicas?"

In the chorus that answered Jessica Rudolph's words, Miss Appleyard could make out Jessica Prud'homme de la Reaux's small voice, squeaking happily, "We'll manage!"

CHAPTER FOUR

The Tower

"Yes, but how *are* we going to manage?" asked Jessica Brown.

The four Jessicas were sitting on the floor in the large, nearly empty room, surveying their new surroundings. It was easy to see why the stigma of special privilege would attach itself to this place; it was certainly the best room in Laurel Dormitory, aside from Mrs. Hayward's.

The large, bright room had cheerful canary-colored wallpaper and white wainscoting. It stood all by itself on the third floor; the rest of the attic was used only for storage. The view was commanding, overlooking the school quadrangle, the lovely hills beyond, the stone wall surrounding Holly Hills, and the evergreen holly bushes that gave the school its name.

As an added feature, the extra flight of stairs Mrs. Hayward had to climb kept her confined to the dormitory's lower levels: the four girls had their room pretty much to themselves. The sophomore Jessicas would be living almost like the senior girls in Hickory where there was very little supervision. The juniors in Laurel dorm were probably green with envy, kicking themselves for not having thought of that wonderful room first.

But first, the problem of their names. How *were* they to manage this absurd situation?

"I just love the fact that everybody's started calling us

'the four Jessicas,' " said Jessica Marshall. "It sets us apart. I'd hate to give that up."

"We don't have to," pointed out Jessica Rudolph. "Here's what I think. On the outside, we present a united front: Jessica, Jessica, Jessica, and Jessica. But when we're by ourselves, each Jessica will have a special name all her own. What do you say?"

"We could try it, I suppose," Jessica Brown said slowly. "It might even work. At home, they call me 'Jessie.' "

"Anybody else laying claim to 'Jessie'?" asked Jessica Rudolph, looking around the room. "No other takers? Good; it's yours."

"I've always kind of liked 'Joss,' " admitted Jessica Marshall, "even though nobody ever called me that."

" 'Joss.' It has a nice ring to it. Everybody in favor?" It was obvious that Jessica Rudolph was accustomed to taking charge.

There was a murmur of assent, and Joss was voted in.

Jessica Prud'homme de la Reaux looked very uncomfortable and blushed as Jessica Rudolph turned her attention to her. "I . . . I . . . never had a nickname," she stammered.

The girls took pity on her obvious embarrassment. "We can afford *one* Jessica, can't we?" asked Jessica Brown.

"Sure," agreed Jessica Marshall.

"All right, by common consent, whenever we're together, the name Jessica is to mean Jessica Prud'homme de la Reaux," said Jessica Rudolph decisively. "And I'll be 'Jody.' Nobody's called me that in years, but I guess it's time to drag the name back out of mothballs. Now, have we all got it straight? To the outside world, we're the four Jessicas, like the Three Musketeers plus One. But up in this room, we'll always be Joss Marshall, Jessie Brown, Jody Rudolph, and Jessica Prud'homme de la Reaux. Agreed?"

"Do we have to sign it in blood?" asked Jessie Brown dryly.

"Don't look at me!" Jody Rudolph put her hands up in mock horror. "I'm overdrawn at the blood bank!" The girls dissolved in laughter.

"Now we have to get serious," said Jody. "If we want to be a lean, mean machine we have to follow certain rules."

"A lean, mean machine?" quavered Jessica Prud' homme de la Reaux in terror.

"Don't worry; I'm not talking about a forty-minute workout." Jody laughed reassuringly. "Listen. What we have here is something different from any other sophomores at Holly Hills. It's a kind of independence, and I propose that we make the most of it. We can turn 'the four Jessicas' into a team, something stronger and better than the four of us individually. It's like training for the Olympics."

Jessie Brown frowned doubtfully. "I'm not sure what you're getting at. I've always functioned pretty well by myself."

"Sure, you have. That's one of your strengths, your independence. Little Jessica here hasn't got a lot of that, and you could help her to get hold of some. That's exactly what I've been talking about. Look, we're in one of the academically toughest schools in America. We all want to go on to good colleges, make something of our lives, carve out future careers for ourselves. Now we have the chance to do it in style. We're all good at something, why not share it? Joss and Jessie are whizzes at science; Jessica knows French inside and out and has already read all the literature we'll need this term; and I can run rings around all of you in mathematics. Why not share the wealth?

"I'm not suggesting we cheat or anything like that," continued Jody. "But if we set up a tutorial/study schedule, with regular hours and regular assignments, each of us lending her own particular strength to the others, we'll all come through with flags flying. It may *seem* like a lot of work, but it will actually cut down our homework hours, and we won't have to do a lot of last-minute cramming before exams, so we'll make the time up then."

"That's a brilliant idea. I'm all for it," applauded Joss.

"I suppose we have nothing to lose," Jessie added cautiously.

"I'd be so happy to help," breathed Jessica.

"That ought to be our first priority," Jody said. "We'll get started as soon as we move our stuff in. I look at it this way. The Apple gave us this room on probation. The faculty will be keeping their eyes on the four Jessicas, and we have to prove that we're worth trusting. The first thing they'll be checking out is our grades. We should show them what the four Jessicas can do."

"Second the motion," called Jessie.

"Third the motion," echoed Joss.

"Fourth it." Jessica made the vote unanimous.

"And that's only the beginning," continued Jody, her freckled face lit up with enthusiasm. "We're going to come out strong, walk tall, and roll right over 'em. A lean, mean machine."

"Can't we just take one thing at a time?" complained Joss Marshall. "I'm exhausted just listening to you."

"You got it." Jody laughed, showing strong white teeth. "But one thing more, only one. What are we going to name this room?"

"Name it?" The others looked blank.

"Don't you think that a place as special as this one deserves a name of its own? What about the Eagle's Nest?"

"No, that's too heavy," protested Jessie. "How about the Rose Garden?"

"Unh-unh, that sounds too much like politics. Any other suggestions?"

"The Tower?" The voice was so soft that they barely heard the words. Jessica Prud'homme de la Reaux was blushing all over, embarrassed to have actually voiced a suggestion out loud.

"The Tower," murmured Jessie Brown. "I like it. It's right, somehow. This place is up high, and private, and filled with fresh air and sunshine. Just like a tower in a fairy tale. Why not?"

"I like it, too," voted Joss.

"And me," added Jody. "The Tower it is, then. Good thinking, Jessica."

Jessica's blush deepened to scarlet, but it was a blush of pride, not embarrassment.

"Okay," said Jody briskly. "We're in business. We have our names, the room has its name, and we're all agreed that we'll form a study group. Now for the next important question. What about boys?"

A good question indeed. What *about* boys? By the rules of Holly Hills, sophomore girls were permitted to date two Saturday nights and two Friday nights in every month. In addition, they could attend the Friday night mixers.

"Mixers" were regularly scheduled chaperoned dances held in the huge dining room. Boys from nearby private schools were loaded into buses and brought to Holly Hills, where the faculty could keep a strict eye on them. The dances were held every second week, with a different boys' school. During the other weeks, busloads of boys would be going to the *other* girls' schools in the area, something like a baseball-game schedule.

Mixers were a mixed blessing. The chaperones were so eagle-eyed about couples dancing too close or slipping off to be alone that it was like being in dancing class. And there was the problem of meeting a great boy one week only to discover he'd met someone he liked better at Briony or Miss Clifford's the week after. Definitely slash-the-throat city.

Once you actually met a boy, it became trickier. Holly Hills was very strict where dating was concerned. Only on one night of the school week was a boy allowed to pay the girl of his choice a visit. He wasn't permitted upstairs, but couples could sit downstairs in the "Goldfish Bowl." There, in full view of everybody coming in and out, you were on display, making self-conscious conversation, but it was better than nothing.

It took a strong-willed boy to last through one of those visits, and not all of them could afford the transportation back and forth between the two schools. Still, love finds a way.

Rules for actually going out on a Friday or Saturday night date were rigid. The boy would have to present a written pass from his own school to the on-duty Holly Hills teacher. Then his date would have to sign out, spelling out for the record the name and school of her escort, the time they checked out, and where they were going. Curfew was eleven P.M. on the dot, and any violation of curfew would result in a girl's being grounded for a month. But even with all the hassle, the girls of Holly Hills managed to fall in love.

Joss Marshall fell in love a lot. Jessie Brown had never been in love. Jessie had attended only one mixer so far, dancing stiffly and grimly with a boy in glasses. He hadn't asked her again. Nor did anybody else. Watching Joss float around the floor as boys fought to cut in, Jessie had sworn off mixers, boys, and other occasions of humiliation.

"I've never been in love," stated Jody. "I never found the time. For years, my life was made up of training and classes and training and practice. Even if my coach and my trainer had let me go out on dates, I was always too tired.''

"Haven't you ever been on a date?'' Joss asked incredulously.

"Sort of. We'd go out in a group, a bunch of us kids, to a movie or down to the beach when we competed in California. But it wasn't a two-by-two thing, most of the time. Some of the boys and girls did get together and pair off, but never me. I guess I never met anybody I liked enough.''

"How about you?'' All eyes turned to little Jessica Prud'homme de la Reaux, who turned bright pink with embarrassment. "Have you ever been in love?''

"Oh, yes,'' replied Jessica surprisingly. "When I was twelve, I fell in love with my algebra tutor. He was so handsome! He reminded me of Mr. Rochester in *Jane Eyre.*''

"That doesn't count,'' Jody protested.

"Yes, it does. Love's love, isn't it?'' Jessie Brown's words were unexpected, especially from so unromantic a source. "If she loved him, why shouldn't it count?''

Jody shrugged. "Okay by me. All I'm saying is that I'd like to make up for some of the time I lost. Lead me to the boys and let me at 'em.''

Joss's eyes narrowed in thought. "There's a mixer this Friday night, Jody, but can you dance with that knee? I have a date this Saturday night, and I could ask him to bring a friend along for you. Mixer or date?''

"Why not both?'' Jody grinned. "I've got a lot of catching up to do. But what about Jessie and Jessica?''

"Not me!'' protested Jessie Brown hastily, putting up one hand in self-defense. "Dating doesn't interest me.''

Jessica's blushes spoke for her more than mere words of protest could do. All she could do was shake her head pleadingly.

"We can't have attitudes like that." Jody tossed her red curls. "What happened to the four Jessicas, the Three Musketeers plus One? What's wrong with going out and having a good time, Jessie?"

"Boys don't excite me. I have five brothers and I see enough of boys at home."

"Brothers aren't boys. They just *look* like boys. I have brothers myself, and believe me, Jessie, boys are better."

Jessie Brown's bony face turned glum. "Well, to tell the bitter truth, it's *me* who doesn't excite them!"

"Now you're talking!" Jody grinned. "And that's where the four Jessicas come in. That's what I meant about lending our strengths to one another. Now why do you suppose Joss is so popular?"

"Ha! That's an easy one! Just look at her!"

"It's true, Jessie, she's pretty. *Very* pretty. But that's not all there is to it. In the first place, not every pretty girl is popular. In the second place, not every popular girl is pretty. In the third place, *you're* a lot prettier than you give yourself credit for. But we'll get to that. Let's stay on the subject of Joss for a minute. Besides being pretty, she likes people, and that includes boys. She welcomes a new face—"

"I'll say I do," interrupted Jessica Marshall, giggling.

"Quiet in the cheap seats," ordered Jody. "Now, as I was saying before I was so rudely interrupted, Joss knows how to talk to boys, how to be friendly. Granted, it may come naturally to her, but sociability is a skill and it can be learned. Joss can teach it to you, and I bet she will. Meanwhile, why don't we work on fixing you up a little, just to let your light shine through?"

"What is this!" Jessie demanded indignantly. "Make-over time? 'Let our editors show you how a simple new hairstyle and a few makeup tricks can make you more vibrant, more self-confident, more attractive to men'?" Her sarcasm didn't fully match the hurt in her eyes.

"Go ahead and yell if you want to," Jody replied mildly. "I don't mind. There's nothing wrong with picking up a tad more self-confidence. Look, Jessie, making the most of yourself isn't one of your strengths, that's all. It *is* one of Joss's. No big deal. There are things about you that we can all learn from, and all I'm saying is that if we pool what we know best and make it available to all of us, then the four Jessicas will be unstoppable! Don't you want to be the best there is?"

"The lean, mean machine, right? Go for the gold, is that it?" retorted Jessie, too caught up in what she was saying to notice Jody flinch away from the reference.

"Why not?" asked Joss suddenly. "Somebody's going to be best, why shouldn't it be the four of us?" She turned to look at her roommate. "Jessie, what Jody is saying makes sense, even when you strip away the locker-room mentality. Life is competitive. To succeed you have to have an edge. Isn't it better for us to help one another get that edge instead of turning our own advantages against each other? Isn't it more blessed to give than to receive?"

Jody held her breath as Jessie turned Joss's words over in her mind.

"Okay," said Jessie finally, and Jody Rudolph let her breath out in a long whoosh. "But what I want to know is how come you're giving the orders all of a sudden? Who died and left you boss?"

Jody smiled brightly. "I was hoping that somebody would ask me that. I admit it, I *have* taken over. I was team captain for too long, I guess. But somebody has to be captain. Anybody else want the job? No? Anytime somebody else wants to take over, just let me know. I'll be happy to step down. And let me make a prediction, right here and now. Sooner or later, all of you will be captain for a while, and it'll happen naturally. We'll be taking turns, I guarantee it. Even little Jessica here.''

The other three turned to look at Jessica Prud'homme de la Reaux, who curled herself up more tightly to present a small target. They'd forgotten about her, just as she'd hoped they would.

"What *about* little Jessica here?'' Jessie wanted to know. "If *I* have to go that mixer, doesn't she?''

"Oh, no!'' squeaked a terrified Jessica. "I couldn't!''

"Jessica's going to take a lot more work than you will,'' said Jody decisively. "I vote that we postpone her debut for a while. All in favor?''

"Aye!'' shrieked little Jessica, breaking the rest of them up.

"Okay, that's settled. We have three days to get Jessie ready, and as much time as we need to get Jessica ready. Joss is already perfect, and I'm going to dive in headfirst, ready or not. Boys, on your guard! Make way for the lean, mean machine or we'll roll right over you! Give me a high five!''

Jody struck her right hand high into the air, and one by one, even little Jessica, the other three leaped to clasp it. It was an important moment for them, one they'd never forget, even after they'd grown to womanhood. The "high five'' signified the real beginning of the four Jessicas.

Of course, at that moment, they had no idea what trouble was on the way.

Of course, at that moment, they had not yet encountered Douglas McVie.

CHAPTER FIVE

Douglas McVie

Every Douglas McVie in the world has the smile of an angel, behind which lurks the heart of a devil. They possess a body that just won't quit. Long legs, narrow waist, shoulders out to *here,* Douglas McVies come equipped with all the optional extras. Plus charm, bushel baskets of charm. Mothers love him and little brothers say he's a good guy. But a good guy he's not. If, by great good fortune (or bad, depending on the point of view) a girl should fall in love with a Douglas McVie, he will run her over, back up and run her over again, leaving his tire tracks all over her wretched body. On the other hand, time spent with a Douglas McVie is never dull.

Douglas McVie was bored. School bored him; it was too easy. Team sports bored him; who wanted to waste time pitting precious competitive energies against muscle-bound jocks? The only sports that appealed to him at all were those that forced him to compete with himself. But it was too early in the year for skiing and too late in the year for sailing; it was too cold and too wet for riding, and he hated tennis. Even girls bored him; there was no challenge anymore.

Most of the glass of the dresser mirror in his room at St. Trinity's was hidden behind photographs of girls—pretty girls, stunning girls, beautiful girls. Most of the photographs bore flowery signatures and embarrassing declarations of love. Douglas was too bored to take them down and throw them away. Whenever he wanted to view the reflection of his own perfection, which was frequently, he'd use the mirror of his roommate's dresser. No photos there.

When Douglas McVie was bored, he became a monster —irritable, vindictive, the terror of the junior dorm. Sophomores quailed at the sight of him, and freshmen actually were known to run away and hide. He was like a mighty volcano, sputtering under the surface, waiting for the right moment to explode and spill hot lava all over everything.

As everybody knows, when the gods of the volcano become angry, the natives sacrifice a virgin to them.

"Say, Doug," said virginal Grady Ferguson, coming into the room he shared with McVie. He found his roommate lounging listlessly on his bed, glaring up at the cracks in the ceiling.

"Don't call me Doug," snarled Douglas. "Use my proper name or address me as *Mr.* McVie."

"All right, *Mr.* McVie. Are we going to the mixer tomorrow night?"

"Where?"

"Holly Hills."

"Sophomores or juniors?"

"Sophomores."

"No way, André. My baby-sitting days are long behind me. I much prefer women to little girls."

"Good, then, I'll go without you. More for me."

"Where's the fire? Why not let them miss you for a few weeks? It'll sharpen their infant appetites. I've told you a thousand times, Ferguson, always leave them hungry for more."

"I want to meet Jessica Rudolph." A look of longing came over Grady's freckled face.

"Jessica the Jock? But she's on crutches! You two planning to go out for the three-legged race?"

"Comical, McVie, you're a laugh riot. Besides, she's not on crutches anymore. I hear she's just using a cane."

"Athletic girls are not my bag, thanks. Too many muscles. None the less, roomie of mine, I wish you joy with your former celebrity. As for me, I prefer less strenuous activity than dragging a girl in a cast around a dance floor. I only exercise when there's a payoff, old buddy. No gain, no pain, that's my motto."

"Well, there's no payoff in the four Jessicas; they don't give, so you can forget that."

Douglas McVie suddenly sat up straight and fixed his dark turquoise eyes on his roommate. "Run that by me one more time, Ferguson," he commanded.

"What?" Grady turned an innocent pair of bright brown eyes to Douglas.

"That part about the four Jessicas. What the hell are the four Jessicas?"

"Haven't you been tuning in to the jungle telegraph? I swear the drums have been beating for two days. Four girls named Jessica in the sophomore class at Holly Hills are rooming together."

Douglas gave a great shout of laughter. "You've gotta be kidding! Do they wear name tags to tell each other apart?"

Grady Ferguson shook his head in exasperation. "I can't talk to you, Ace," he exclaimed impatiently. "You're never serious."

"No, no, go on." Douglas choked his laughter back and did his best to keep his face straight, but his mind was racing with the possibilities. "Are they gorgeous?"

"Well, Jessica Marshall is a real beauty, I danced with her a couple of times at the freshman mixers last year, when you didn't condescend to put in an appearance. And you've seen photographs of Jessica Rudolph. She's got a great smile, and a sensational body."

"Is she the girl on the cover of *Sports Illustrated* you've got Scotch-taped inside your closet door where I wouldn't find it and call you on it, you turkey?" Douglas had the satisfaction of seeing his roommate turn bright pink with embarrassment.

"Okay, one beauty and one jock. What about the other two?" demanded Douglas.

"I don't know," admitted Grady. "But I intend to find out. Coming with me tomorrow night?"

Douglas McVie thought hard. Four girls, all named Jessica! This was a real challenge, too good to pass up. It was like a Shakespearean comedy, four heroines and one hero. Himself, of course. Suddenly, he was no longer bored. His grin widened, and his face took on a beatific glow. He was never more evil than when he appeared most angelic. Now he was looking like a choirboy.

"No, m'boy, I think I'll give it the old El Paso, and send you instead. Search-and-destroy mission, take no prisoners. Make them all adore you, Ferguson. Bring me their lovely heads back on a platter."

"You're bizarre, Doug, you know that? Totally bizarre."

"I want a full report on those Jessicas. Don't leave out a single petty detail. Pile on the data, age, height, weight stripped, sexual preferences, favorite color, that kind of thing. As for me, I'll just stay home and knit."

Grady shrugged his shoulders. "Suit yourself."

Douglas McVie pushed his long legs over the side of the bed and pulled himself lazily to his feet. Loping over to Ferguson's mirror, he took inventory, examining his cleft chin, his handsome profile, the waves in his reddish-brown hair. Four Jessicas. Interesting. But he needed time to think about it. No one rushes into an adventure without some preparation. He batted his thick eyelashes at himself and peered long and lovingly into his blue-green eyes.

Four Jessicas. Mmmmmmmmm.

Yes, that would be his project for his junior year. A biology project, so to speak. He would make all four of those little lovelies fall in love with him, one right after the other. It would be amusing. But how to go about it?

Then the answer came to him, loud and clear. *Divide and conquer!*

CHAPTER SIX

Making Jessie Over

For the next three days, as soon as classes were dismissed for the afternoon, the four Jessicas gathered in the Tower to "do Jessie Brown over." This mainly took the form of much excited talking and interrupting; even so, a number of positive things emerged from these sessions.

"Please don't try to make me into somebody I'm not," pleaded Jessie.

"Don't worry. We're going to make you into somebody you *are* but don't recognize yet. This will be the inner you," Jody Rudolph assured her.

They went rummaging through her wardrobe with little cries of disappointment. Pickings were pretty slim.

"Do you call these things jeans?" Jody held them up and stared at them in disbelief.

"No, as a matter of fact I call them dungarees, and I usually wear them when I'm washing the car at home."

"Good choice." Jody nodded. "Any reason they're so loose and baggy?"

"They're more comfortable that way. Besides"—Jessie's eyes fell and she looked uncomfortable—"I don't like wearing tight things. I'm so *skinny*!"

Speechless, Jody Rudolph cast her eyes up to heaven, while Joss Marshall tried her best to stifle her laughter, and failed.

"Jessie, don't you know that thin is in? There's no such thing as skinny anymore. Women are throwing away thousands of dollars at famous fat farms in the vain hope of attaining bodies like yours.''

"Tens of thousands," chimed in Jessica Prud'homme de la Reaux.

"Well, my brothers always tease me about being all bones and no meat. Honestly, I tried to put on weight. I eat like a horse, stuff myself on French fries, brownies, and Coke, but I never seem to gain an ounce!"

Jody curled her hands into claws. "Kill, *kill*!" she yipped. "Just let me get at her throat! It's no fair! There *you* are, feeding your face with hot fudge, while *I* have to count every lettuce leaf that goes into my mouth! Do you realize that I've put on eight pounds since my accident?" It was true; Jody was recognizably heavier than the sylph on the cover of *Sports Illustrated*.

Little Jessica was rummaging around in one of her suitcases. "Here, try these on!" she called. "I never ever wore them, not even once."

"These" were a very small pair of impeccably cut jeans with an impeccable designer label. "They're not really my style." Jessica smiled shyly. "I'd love for you to have them."

"Wow, will you look at those?" Joss breathed reverently. "What are they? Size minus two?"

"Even *I* won't fit into those." Jessie shook her head. "They're cut for a seven-year-old."

"Not standing up you won't," agreed Jody Rudolph briskly. "Lie down!"

"Say what?"

"Lie down! Right here, flat on the floor. Now take off your skirt. Come on, Jessie, *do* it! Good. Now I'll just slip the legs on. Good. Now wiggle!"

"Wiggle?"

"Yes, wiggle into them. Pretend it's aerobics. It *is*

aerobics! Wiggle, damn it! Yes, that's right, keep wriggling. They're moving, they're moving! They're almost halfway there!'' The other girls gathered around as Jessie struggled, wiggled, and bumped her way into the skin tight jeans.

"Snap them! Snap them!" yelled little Jessica excitedly, her face flushed with happiness, timidity forgotten. "You did it!"

Jessie lay back panting. "I'm wiped," she gasped.

"Now stand up and let's see you," ordered Jody.

"Stand up? Are you real? I *can't* stand up! These things are way too tight. I can hardly breathe, let alone stand up."

"They'll give. Denim always gives. In a year or two they'll actually be comfortable. Help her up, girls." Jody pounded her cane on the floor in approval as the others pushed and pulled a perspiring Jessie Brown to her feet. "You look like dynamite!"

"I feel like an idiot."

"Il faut souffrir pour atteindre la beauté." Little Jessica smiled. "One must suffer to be beautiful. Come see, Jessie." Jessica pulled her over to the full-length mirror that hung inside the closet door. For a moment, Jessie regarded herself in silence.

The French jeans hugged her long thighs and clung to her hips like a second skin. Her body, which seemed to be "too skinny" all Jessie's life was now fashionable— narrow hips, concave belly, small buttocks.

Jessie stood up straighter. Her good old Shetland sweater outlined her strong shoulders and skimmed her small waist, making her appear even thinner. She looked good. In fact, she looked terrific. The horribly expensive jeans were a resounding success. She turned from the mirror with the broadest smile that Joss Marshall, who'd been her friend all through freshman year, had ever seen on her. "Are you really able to part with these, Jessica?" she asked.

"Oh, yes! I have more clothes than I know what to do with, and they never fit me the way they fit you. I'm *happy* to give them to you! *Please* take them!"

"Thank you," Jessie said with a hug. "I accept with gratitude."

"Now those dungarees can go back to washing cars for a living," joked Jody. "But we still have to get you ready for Friday night. No jeans at the mixers. The rules say skirts or dresses. Back to the closet."

Jessie Brown's wardrobe was skimpy and practical. Her mother had purchased her school outfits with years of wear in mind. All of Jessie's skirts were made of solid iron with deep hems. A couple of dresses, suitable for chapel on Sunday, would disappear into the wallpaper at a dance. At the back of the closet hung an ancient tweed jacket.

"What's this?"

"That's my brother Scott's old jacket. He outgrew it."

"It's good," Jody said thoughtfully, her head on one side. "It has distinct possibilities."

"*That* old thing?" Jessie Brown could barely believe what she was hearing.

"Sure." Joss took the jacket from Jody. "It's Brooks Brothers, says so right here on the label. That means the older the better. Old money, don'cha know." She stuck her tiny nose in the air and tried to look snobbish, succeeding only in appearing comical.

"Trust me," commanded Jody Rudolph. "It is très chic to wear boys' clothes if you're not a boy. By any chance, do you have one of Scott's button-down shirts, preferably Brooks, preferably pink?"

"Somewhere in the bottom drawer . . ."

"Aha!" Joss Marshall waved a pink shirt in the air and handed it to Jody. "The right stuff!"

Jody was sniffing the shirt. "Smells like boy," she commented. "Wash it and iron it and we'll have it smelling like girl in no time. You haven't got a necktie of Scott's, by any chance?"

"No, nor his athletic supporter either!" cried Jessie, stung. "What on earth would I do with one of his neckties?"

"You'd knot it loosely and wear it with the knot pulled down to the third button. It's really cute. But never mind. You've got a good strong neck and pretty skin. We'll just unbutton the top three . . . or maybe four buttons."

"No chance, Sundance! I'm not going into that mixer to flash tit at St. Trinity's!"

"Language, language," chided Jody, smiling rosily. "We'll see when the times comes. Now, okay, we've got the top half taken care of. What about the bottom half? Don't you have anything besides those depressing skirts? They look like prison matrons' uniforms!"

"Too bad she can't stay in those jeans," mourned Joss.

"I may *have* to stay in them, because I'm not so sure I can get *out* of them," grumbled Jessie somewhat sourly.

"Can you produce something else wonderful from that treasure chest of yours?" Jody asked Jessica. "You're closest to Jessie's size."

"No, now, wait a minute!" Jessie protested. "I'm no charity case." But little Jessica was already pulling the heavy suitcase out from under the bed again and flinging it open.

"Help yourself!" she said, and grinned from ear to ear.

At once, Joss Marshall knelt beside her and began to turn over the contents. Never in her life had she handled such beautiful and expensive fabrics. Cottons poured through her hands like silk, and the thin wools were nearly as transparent as gauze.

"Look! What about this?" she asked, holding up a soft pearly gray wool skirt with a belted waistline. It was cut on the bias so that the trumpet pleats belled out like flower petals. Very simple, very expensive, very beautiful.

"I think she's got it, by George she's got it!" Jody chuckled. "Try it on, Jessie. Try it on with the shirt and jacket."

It took two of them to peel her out of the jeans, but at last Jessie Brown stood posing nervously in front of her roommates, waiting for their comments. They studied her in silence. The skirt was much shorter on her tall figure than it would have been on little Jessica, and it swirled around her knees, revealing her long, coltish legs.

"What do you think?" Joss asked Jody at last.

"Yes, for heaven's sake say something!" cried Jessie. "Before I turn to stone!"

"The outfit's good," Jody said slowly, "although the hair and the face still need work. The shirt has to be washed and ironed, and the jacket and skirt steam-pressed. We can hang them in the shower. Yes, I like the look, Jessie. It's casual, comfortable, and right for you. There's no sense in trying to turn you into a centerfold; the effect we're trying to achieve here is class. We're getting there. It's rough going, but we're getting there."

"You're not going to change my hair or face! I'm warning you!" Jessie had her back up, and her dark gray eyes glinted like steel.

"Not *change*, dummy," Joss said soothingly. "*Enhance!*" Her eyes narrowed again in thought. "Do you always wear your hair that way, hanging down your back in one braid?" She picked the heavy braid up in her small hand. The hair was lustrous and very dark, like the satin fur of a well-fed cat.

At once, Jessie snatched her braid back out of Joss's hands.

"If you're thinking of cutting it . . ." she growled.

"No! I forbid it!" They turned, surprised. Jessica Prud'homme de la Reaux, her usually gentle eyes snapping, was facing them down like a tiny mother tiger.

"Hey, back off!" Joss laughed. "We're not going to cut it!"

Little Jessica looked embarrassed. "It's only that Jessie's hair is so beautiful," she said quietly. "I've always dreamed of long, straight hair like that, instead of this frizzy mop of mine."

"Don't worry, we're not going to do anything radical to Jessie's hair. Only, I was thinking, do you ever take it out of its braid?" asked Jody.

"You mean, wear it loose, just hanging down my back?"

"Something like that."

"Not since I was in grade school. There's just so much of it, it gets flyaway and messy."

"I'm sure it's lovely," murmured Jessica. "But I have a sort of . . . idea. We once had a *bonne,* a maid who dressed hair beautifully. She did my mother's hair. My mother had hair very much like yours, Jessie, very long and very thick and dark. What Yvonne did was to loosen some of the strands in the front, just like so, and curl them so that they made beautiful tendrils all around Mama's face. She left the rest loose, hanging down her back to her waist. She was so very beautiful—" The girl's voice broke, and tears filled her eyes. That beautiful mother had died ten years ago, when Jessica was only four.

Jessica Brown put one arm around Jessica Prud'homme de la Reaux and hugged her tightly. "That's a wonderful idea," she said gently. "I'd like to try that."

"You can use my hot rollers," volunteered Jessica Marshall.

"I'll lend you my pink lipstick," added Jessica Rudolph. "It's the same color as your shirt. A little lipstick is all you need. You'll be sensational looking."

"Well, at least I'll be comfortable. I hate getting all dressed up like a trick monkey. If a boy wants to take me out, it should be because he likes *me,* not my clothes."

"Never underestimate the power of a great outfit," advised Jody. "Boys are as impressionable as girls, you know. You can fake 'em out by your threads, at least at first meeting. In the war between men and women, the opening skirmish is crucial, and the right clothes are a definite tactical advantage."

"Okay, General, you win!" Jessie laughed, throwing her hands up in the air in mock surrender. "But that's enough for today, really. Now that we've got the weapons, can we leave the rest for tomorrow? We still have one more day before the dance."

"Dis-*missed*!" Jody laughed back. "Tomorrow we'll cover that all-important topic of What to Talk about on the First Date. Which, of course, will be Joss's assignment, since she's the only one of us who's ever had a real date. As for you, little Jessica, I'm very proud of you. Not only did you help Jessie out in every way, but you were able to stand up to the rest of us. I'm promoting you to corporal, no, sergeant!"

At these words of praise from her idol, Jessica Prud'homme de la Reaux blushed deeply and happily. It was true; she had completely forgotten her timidity. Maybe there was hope for her after all.

CHAPTER SEVEN

First Time Out

By the time that six buses had delivered their eager loads of hot-to-trot St. Trinity boys to Holly Hills that Friday night, three of the Jessicas were as ready as they'd ever be.

Joss, who looked magnificent in any old thing she threw on, had thrown on a simple cashmere sweater and tweed skirt and looked magnificent. The pale yellow of her hair against the russet of the sweater was a touch of autumn, of beautiful leaves turning red and gold. Even Joss, who was usually pretty cool around boys, having cut her teeth on their hearts, felt her pulses racing. It had already been three weeks since she had fallen out of love, which was something of a record for her. Who knew what tonight would bring? There were a hundred boys down there tonight, and one of them might just be that special person for her. Maybe this time, it might even last.

Jody, who was still limping around on her cane, had dressed with care. Her wardrobe was almost entirely new, because she had put on weight since the accident and couldn't squeeze into her favorite dresses. But the dress she had chosen, a simple navy-blue jersey with a small white collar; was slenderizing and becoming and showed off her bouncy red curls to advantage. As an accessory, Jody had wrapped a jaunty red ribbon around the white knee cast and tied it in a bow.

Jessie, wearing Jessica's skirt and her brother's shirt and jacket, couldn't get over her reflection in the mirror.

Another person, a completely and totally different person stared back at her in wonderment. This person had large gray eyes and long, beautiful dark hair. Little Jessica Prud'homme de la Reaux had spent almost an hour putting in the hot rollers, taking them out, and arranging the soft tendrils that framed Jessie's face. Suddenly, as if by magic, Jessie's face had been transformed from its skinny old self to a perfect example of superb bone structure. Jody scrounged around the dorm and came up with a silk striped necktie, which she knotted loosely under the shirt collar.

Jessie had objected to wearing three shirt buttons open but had settled on two; the tie knot hung down to the middle of her shirt and emphasized her long, slender neck.

"Wow!" breathed Jody, stepping back to view the effect of her labors.

"Wow!" echoed Joss sincerely.

Little Jessica said nothing, but her eyes grew huge and round in admiration, and her baby lips curved in a smile.

Jessie had to agree. "Wow!" was the word. And the best part of it was that she felt natural in her clothes, not dressed up like a poodle at a dog show. If only she felt *inside* the way she looked *outside*! She might appear to be oozing self-confidence but underneath she was still just plain Jessie Brown from a small town on the Maine coast, a girl with five brothers and no romance in her soul.

Still, she'd never looked so good in her life. *That* was something.

Jessie turned from the mirror. "Thanks, Jessicas," she said warmly. "I mean it. Thanks."

It was time to go. Across the grassy quad, in the dining room stripped of its tables and decorated for the dance, the boys of St. Trinity were already waiting for their dancing partners. The evening was young and filled with promise.

Three Jessicas turned to the fourth, inviting her to join

them. But little Jessica Prud'homme de la Reaux shook her head vehemently and snuggled more deeply into the window seat, where she was fighting the Trojan War at the side of Achilles and Hector. Waving her copy of *The Iliad* at her friends, she called out, "Have a wonderful time! And *bonne chance!*" But as the door closed behind the three of them she felt suddenly very lonely, and a tear dropped onto the page, right into the middle of a battle.

Grady Ferguson had maneuvered himself into position where he could see every girl coming in through the door, but he had been pushed aside from the doorway itself by eager St. Trinity juniors taller and stronger than he was. He knew he had to bring back complete descriptions of the four Jessicas to Douglas McVie, or McVie would kill him.

Well, maybe not *kill* him, but he'd never let Grady forget he'd screwed up. One thing for sure, a pissed-off Douglas McVie was no pleasure to have around.

Grady himself had his heart set on only one of them— Jessica Rudolph, or "Jessica the Jock," as she was already known around St. Trinity. It wasn't her fame that attracted him, although nobody sneezed at a magazine cover; it was her wonderful smile that had made him paste her picture up behind his closet door—that smile, and the courage she had shown after the accident, when she saw all her hard work and hopes go down the tubes. What he felt for her wasn't pity, it was warm sympathy that made him want to comfort her.

Apparently, he wasn't alone in that feeling. Here came three of the Jessicas now, right through the door. The girls were being mobbed, especially the little redhead in the middle.

Jessica Rudolph.

Grady felt his heart turn over at the sight of her. She was different looking somehow . . . heavier, that was it!

Almost plump, but Grady didn't mind. He liked a girl with a little meat on her bones. The smile was the same, and so was the courage. Jessica Rudolph stood leaning on her cane, grinning at the boys surrounding her, chatting easily, wearing a bright red ribbon tied around her knee cast. What a girl!

Quickly, his thoughts still on Jody, he memorized the other two so that Douglas could debrief him later. Jessica Marshall he recognized immediately. Who wouldn't? She was a cotton-candy blonde, with fluffy hair, a pair of eyes that could knock a man's socks off, and a gorgeous bod.

The other girl he'd never seen before, but she was something to see. Tall and thin, she could have passed for a fashion model, with incredible hair and eyes that sparkled clear across the room. He loved the way she was dressed; he owned a jacket exactly like the one she was wearing. But which Jessica was she? Jessica Brown or Jessica Prud'homme de la Reaux? He'd better find out. And where was the fourth Jessica? He'd better find that out, too, or he'd never hear the end of it from McVie.

He tried to get closer to the girls, especially to Jody, but the mob scene around the three Jessicas was too much for him; it was like trying to break through a stone wall. Grady's heart sank and he started to become desperate. He *had* to meet Jessica Rudolph! She was the girl he'd waited for all his seventeen years. But how was he supposed to break through those linebackers?

Suddenly an idea occurred to him, and he slipped out of the room as unobtrusively as he could. One minute he was there, the next he was gone.

Jessie Brown hadn't been surrounded by so many boys since her brothers had brought their scout troops home for a cookout. But those boys had treated her with all the familiarity of a sister, while these boys were begging her to dance. She couldn't get over it!

She'd naturally expected that Joss and Jody would be rushed, so that came as no surprise. But that she herself would be the object of so much male attention was beyond Jessie's comprehension!

As she danced off with a tall boy in a school blazer, her mind was spinning. She responded automatically to his questions—her name, where she came from, what she was studying—but her thoughts were elsewhere. She didn't even catch his name or look up into his face, although she was dimly aware that it was quite a nice face.

What was going on here? Yesterday Little Orphan Annie and today Cinderella. Could a couple of hot rollers and some pale pink lipstick make so much difference? Or was it because these boys wanted to use her as a stepping-stone to the more beautiful Joss or the more famous Jody? Or was it something entirely different? Did it, perhaps, have to do with the way she felt about herself? Standing tall instead of slouching? Smiling instead of scowling? Could that be it, something as simple as that?

Yesterday, Joss had given her Lesson One in "How to Talk to a Boy."

"All those cute magazines tell you to talk about *his* interests," Joss had told her gravely. "Forget it; it's boring, it's deadly, and it's very, very transparent. Plus it's the easiest way to make a fool of yourself. Talk about the things *you* know about, the subjects in which you shine. Sooner or later you'll hit on one he's interested in, and then the two of you can have a real conversation."

"Great," Jessie had replied glumly. "You're telling me to shine, and I can't even get up a glimmer."

"Sometimes you make me so mad I could strangle you with my bare hands. Actually, I would, but I just did my nails! You turkey, you know everything there is to know about sailing and fishing and tennis, not to mention microbiology! You love music—talk to him about Mozart and Madonna! You have definite ideas about politics; if I hear you lecture about world hunger one more time, I'm going to give up eating. As long as you're trying for a boy, why not try for an intelligent one?''

It had seemed like good advice at the time, but right now she was too nervous to follow it.

Suddenly, Jessie became uncomfortably aware that the boy she was dancing with had said something to her. Blushing a deep red, she looked up at him.

''Pardon? I'm afraid I didn't catch what you said.''

''What I said was, 'You look as if you're a thousand miles away,' and I guess I was right.'' He had a thick accent that Jessie could define only vaguely as ''southern.''

Despite herself, Jessie smiled. ''I guess you were. Sorry. I'll try to do better.''

''I don't really mind.'' The boy smiled down at her. ''You're like a princess in a far-off tower, beautiful and remote.''

Nobody had ever, ever said anything even distantly resembling that to Jessica Brown. Ever. She stopped dancing to catch her breath, then looked up into that nice face again, that *very* nice face.

''Actually I *do* live in a tower.'' She smiled. ''Tell you what. I have an idea. Let's go back to square one and start all over again. How do you do? My name is Jessica Brown and I'm a sophomore at Holly Hills.''

''How do *you* do? My name is Alexander Edwards and I'm a junior at St. Trinity. Lovely weather we're having, don't you think?''

Laughing, they danced off together, and Jessie was astonished at how simple it could be, falling in . . . like.

* * *

Jody couldn't get a word in edgewise. There were so many boys around her, all talking at once, demanding her attention. She sat on the sidelines, watching the dancers from the most comfortable chair they could find for her. Boys were perched around her everywhere, each one better looking than the next. If this is a dream, then Mom, don't wake me up, she thought.

This was what she missed all those years, always in training, always seeing other girls going out on dates, while her only dates were with the parallel bars. Now, out of gymnastic action, she'd found another entirely different kind of action.

But which boy to choose? It was confusing, like the menu of a fancy restaurant, with too many chef's specials and all of them delicious. Even though she was a cheeseburger-and-fries girl at heart, Jody was tempted to pig out. She wanted them all.

Wait a minute. Who on earth is that? A boy was limping toward her, leaning on a stick. His right knee was wrapped up in a lumpy white bandage, around which was tied his necktie! For a minute, Jody felt a stab of rage flash through her; it was a perfect parody of herself, bow and all!

But then she saw the grinning face covered with even more freckles than hers, the bright, brown merry eyes, heard him saying, "One side, please. Let me through. Football injury; they got me on the two-yard line, but I made the touchdown anyway. One side, please. Hero coming through."

And she burst into laughter.

Snagging the chair next to hers, Grady fell into it with an exaggerated sigh of relief. "Ah, that's better! Now the agony will subside."

"You dork!" Jody giggled. "That's not a bandage!"

"No," he confessed. "It's my undershirt, rolled up. And I swiped the stick off a blackboard in one of the class-rooms. If you tell on me, they'll send me to Devil's Island for life, like Steve McQueen and Dustin Hoffman. I can't even swim! You won't tell on me, will you? Not you, kind lady. I kees the hem of your garment." And he reached for her dress.

"Touch me and die!" Jody laughed, raising her cane in the air and waving it in mock menace.

All around them, the other boys began to melt away two and three at a time, off to find other girls and salvage what remained of the dance. Grady's prayers had been answered. They were by themselves, the two of them. He was alone with Jessica Rudolph, if being in the same room with several hundred teenagers and a dozen or more chaperons is your definition of *alone*.

"Grady Ferguson, at milady's service."

"Jessica Rudolph."

"No kidding? *The* Jessica Rudolph? The radical chocolate-chip-cookie baker and world-class Frisbee freak? Wow, I'm destroyed!" Grady clutched at his chest and pretended to stagger.

"You squid!" Jody was laughing so hard her ribs ached. "What got you so psyched that you dressed up like Halloween and hobbled over here like Igor?"

"Take another look, lady. You're lookin' at one hundred thirty pounds of slack flab. Do you actually think I could have broken through that mongo backfield you had surrounding you if I didn't have a shtick? Hey, that's a good one, shtick, stick, get it?"

"I got it, Ferguson, but I don't want it. Wrap that joke in newspaper, put it out for the sanitation department, pray we don't get a summons, and that the dog doesn't eat it and die."

"Poetry, Rudolph, sheer poetry. Do they allow you to dance?"

"I *can* dance a little, Slick, but why would I want to?"

"To feel my arms around you, why else?"

"That's the worst offer I've had all night. Correction, that's the worst offer I've had in sixteen years!"

Nevertheless, with a slight assist from Grady, Jody rose to her feet. Leaning her weight partly on him and partly on her cane, she moved very slowly with him around a small piece of the dance floor.

They didn't speak, but he rested his cheek on her curly hair and tightened his hand at her waist. Jessica Rudolph felt such a singing in her chest she thought she would burst with happiness.

Jessica Prud'homme de la Reaux was fast asleep on the window seat when the other three came in, but she sat up when the light went on and rubbed her eyes.

"Did you have a good time?" She yawned.

"If you call perfection a good time." Jody grinned.

"You met somebody!" Little Jessica's face lit up eagerly.

"Well, I guess I sort of did. A flaky kid named Grady Ferguson. More freckles than me; maybe that's why I like him. Anyway, he makes me laugh."

"How was it for you, Jessie?"

Jessica Brown blushed. "I had a surprisingly good time, I have to admit. Thank heaven for hot rollers."

"But did you meet anybody?" little Jessica persisted.

Jessica hesitated. "I danced with a few boys, and they all seemed nice. One of them . . ." Her voice trailed off uncertainly.

"*Oui?*" prompted Jessica, so fascinated that she unconsciously lapsed into French.

Shrugging, Jessie frowned. "Oh, I don't know. He comes from Virginia, and I could hardly understand him sometimes. The soft way he talks is so different from what I was used to in Maine. But he was very nice . . . Alex. Alexander Edwards."

"Did he ask you out?" Joss demanded. By now all the girls had their pajamas on and were taking turns in the bathroom.

Jessie shook her head. Her face looked suddenly despondent. "He won't," she predicted gloomily.

"He will," promised Joss. "I can feel it in my bones. He'll call. And even if he doesn't, so what? There are plenty of other boys. After all, tonight was really your first time out."

Jessie hadn't realized until this moment how much she wanted Alex Edwards to call for a date.

"How about you, Joss? Did you fall in love again tonight?" teased Jody.

Jessica Marshall shook her golden head. "Nope. I had a good time, but . . . I don't know . . . something was missing. There just wasn't anybody special."

"Joss is getting jaded," commented Jessie. "Ordinary boys just aren't good enough for her. Wait and see. She'll wind up with Tom Cruise or Tom Selleck or Tom Berenger or Tom Hanks one of these days."

"How'd you like to eat a towel?" growled Joss.

"I'm telling you there were only three of them there, McVie. What do you want me to do, pull the fourth Jessica out of a hat?"

"Run them down for me again. Jessica Brown?"

"Tall, thin, very elegant looking, like a thoroughbred horse or a greyhound. Gorgeous hair. I didn't dance with her, but she was out on the floor all evening. Very popular. Edwards danced with her about ten times."

"Sounds tasty. Jessica Marshall?"

"I can't believe you never met her, Doug. She's one of the prettiest girls at Holly Hills. All pink and white and gold. But smart too."

"Oh, I'll meet her, m'boy, you can bet on that. And Jessica Prud'homme de la Unpronounceable never showed up?"

Grady shook his head. "Not that I saw, or anybody else for that matter. Mabye she had another date."

"More likely she had a cold. What female in her right mind would forgo a St. Trinity mixer for a mere Broadway play or dinner at the Four Seasons? We're the cream of the cream, my boy, the most desirable lads in creation. Just bear that in mind the next time some girl has her foot on your neck and you're pleading for mercy. And now, the piece of resistance. Miss *Sports Illustrated* herself. What about Jessica Rudolph?"

Grady turned away, refusing to answer, his mouth set in a stubborn line.

Douglas McVie raised one shapely eyebrow and regarded his roommate attentively. "I said," he repeated with care, "what about Jessica Rudolph?"

"Damn you, McVie!" shouted Grady angrily, two spots of color dyeing his cheeks red. His hands were clenched into fists. "You just forget about Jessica Rudolph!"

Douglas smiled. "So that's how the land lies," he said softly. "My best friend and roommate Mr. Grady Ferguson is in love, is he?"

Grady opened his mouth to protest, then shut it without a word. He nodded miserably.

"Yes, Ace, I think I am."

But as the thought of it hit him hard and sank right in, he brightened. "You bet I am!" he yelled happily. "I'm in love with Jessica Rudolph!"

Tough toenails, thought Douglas McVie, even as he pounded his roommate on the back in congratulations. Sorry to have to do this to you, Grady m'boy, but I don't want to break up the set. If there are four, I want four. And I'll get them too. It's only a matter of time.

CHAPTER EIGHT

Simon

Almost the very moment she first arrived at Holly Hills, before she picked up her room assignment or unpacked her bags, Jessica Marshall had signed up for riding on Saturday afternoons. The fact that horseback riding was available as an optional extra was one deciding factor in Joss's selecting Holly Hills to begin with. For her to be without a horse was unthinkable.

Actually, she didn't want to leave Wyoming or the ranch or her parents, but most of all she wanted to stay with Moonlight Sonata, her palomino gelding. Parting with him was one of the most difficult things she had ever done in her life. They'd grown up together; they had been inseperable. Joss was certain that he missed her as much as she missed him, and hoped that he wouldn't go off his feed without her. He was getting on in years.

Although Holly Hills had no stables of its own, there was a stable the girls could use nearby, with a series of good riding trails that ranged over the hills and through lovely woodlands. In order to ride, girls had to be carefully tested and graded at first. Beginners rode as a group, with a riding teacher; intermediates were allowed to go out in pairs; their range was a little wider. As an advanced rider, expert in the saddle, Jessica Marshall was allowed to ride alone and had the run of the trails. The only restriction on her was time. No more than three hours. They always passed like three minutes.

When the four Jessicas had made up their tutorial and
study schedules, it was understood from the beginning that
nothing could keep Joss Marshall from her ride on fine
days. Later in the semester, when the weather would turn
icy and wet, she'd be forced to stay in on Saturday afternoons with the rest of her roomies, but in the lovely crisp
days of September and October, the crunch of leaves under
a horse's hooves, the grassy smell of a horse's breath, and
the comforting feel of its sturdy body under the saddle
were all it took to make her happy.

Joss had ridden just about every horse the stable could
provide, settling at last on a spirited young mare named
Mabel. Sitting on Mabel's back as the horse picked its
delicate way through the forest undergrowth, knowing that
they'd soon be out on flat country and galloping together,
Joss felt her spirits rising. The academic hassles and the
troubles of the past week slipped from her shoulders like
an old discarded sweater.

But the sound of another horse's hooves behind her
brought a frown to her brow. She was so careful to avoid
the other girls who rode. These moments alone on horseback were the most private and most precious of the week,
and she didn't want to share them with anybody, especially
not with inferior riders. Digging her heels into Mabel's
side, Joss flicked her lightly with the reins, hurrying her
toward open country.

Behind her, the sound of the hooves came nearer.

She was out in the open now, and the horse broke free,
running as swiftly as white water, stirring Joss's blood.
This was the purest bliss; a healthy fast horse to ride on a
cool and lovely day.

The other rider was drawing closer. If she pushed Mabel
any harder, the mare might suffer for it. The best thing to
do was rein in and see where the other rider was going,
then head off in the opposite direction. Joss tugged on the

reins, pulling the horse's head up and slowing her to a stop. Then she turned.

The most handsome man she'd ever seen was riding toward her on a chestnut gelding. He sat tall and straight in the saddle, riding easily, the wind lifting his thick, wavy hair and swirling it around his head. For an instant, Joss's heart stopped.

The man smiled and waved his hand, and Joss found herself smiling and waving back.

When he had almost reached her side, he reined in, draping the reins over the pommel of his English saddle. Up close, Joss could see that he was really a boy, not a man, perhaps seventeen or eighteen years old. What had fooled her from a distance was that he had the body of a man, broad-shouldered and deep-chested. His hair was tousled and his eyes were the color of the ocean when the sun shines on it.

"Hi!" He grinned. Naturally, he had a cleft chin. Not one detail had been left out.

"Hi!" answered Joss rather weakly.

"Mind if I ride along with you? I saw you leaving the stable, and since it was such a great day for a ride, I was hoping you wouldn't object to company." He spoke easily, without awkwardness or shyness, as though it would be the most natural thing in the world for the two of them to ride together.

Joss hesitated. As attractive as he was, this boy was a stranger to her. She didn't even know his name. Even his horse was unfamiliar to her, although she thought she knew every horse in the livery stable.

As if he were reading her thoughts, he smiled again, holding out his hand. "My name is Slattery. Simon Slattery."

"Jessica Marshall." She shook his hand.

Their horses had taken the opportunity to graze a little

on the thin autumn grass. As Simon Slattery's gelding bent his head to nibble, the boy, without thinking, stroked the horse's neck with long, gentle fingers.

There was such affection and sweetness about the instinctual gesture that, seeing it, Joss Marshall fell instantly in love.

Simon Slattery! Even the name evoked a shiver, not to mention his tousled hair and broad shoulders.

"Are you a Holly Hills girl?" he was asking.

For an instant, she was afraid she wouldn't be able to utter a syllable, but she managed to croak a "yes," and then it got easier.

"Are you from one of the schools around here?" she asked as their horses began to move side by side at a gentle pace.

Grinning ruefully at her, Simon shook his head. "Nope. Nothing that fancy for the Slatterys. I'm a senior at Rogers High in Kenton."

Kenton was thirty miles away, the biggest town close to Holly Hills. Joss's heart sank. Holly Hills did not encourage their girls to mix with boys who were not from the private-school network. There was no mechanism set up for control. The boys of Chalfont and St. Trinity and the other schools had to obtain passes, they had a curfew, they were, in fact, "registered" as okay with Holly Hills.

But the townies, who could come and go as they pleased, without written permission or curfews, posed a genuine threat to the school authorities, whose job it was to guard and protect the girls' private as well as academic lives.

Yet this boy riding beside her in his faded jeans, his shirt collar open to expose a strong, sun-browned throat, moved her as none of the boys she had been "in love" with earlier had done. This was the real thing. Love at first sight; a cliché, perhaps, but an overwhelming one.

She had a momentary vision of how right they must look

together, two good-looking young people on horseback, but dismissed the thought as trivial. What she was feeling went beyond mere appearances. Still, the fact that Simon was so very handsome certainly didn't hurt.

"What's your horse's name?" she asked.

"Thunderbird. Yours?"

"Mabel." And they laughed. Thunderbird and Mabel, what an absurd team!

"Is he yours?"

"Uh, no. I wish he were. No, I only take him out on Saturday afternoons sometimes."

Saturday afternoon, sometimes! Then there *was* a chance that she might see him again!

"You ride like you were born on horseback," Simon told her appreciatively.

"I just about was." Joss laughed. And then she told him everything—about the little horse ranch in Wyoming, about those awful winters when they were totally snowed in and she had to take her classes over local television, about her beloved palomino. When she mentioned Moonlight Sonata's name, tears came into her eyes.

Simon reached one strong hand over, took hers, and squeezed it tightly in sympathy. Joss felt her heart turn over in her chest.

Suddenly, she wanted him to kiss her, to hold her in his arms and press her against him tightly and cover her lips with his. She'd kissed a lot of boys, but it was mostly because *they* wanted to. Now it was *her* turn to want.

"How about a race?" he asked her suddenly.

Joss looked doubtful. "I'm not sure that Mabel is up to racing Thunderbird."

"How about only to that sycamore tree over there?" It was about two hundred yards off.

"You're on!"

Joss kicked Mabel lightly in the flanks and they were

off, raising dust under the horses' hooves, flying neck and neck like lightning across the meadow.

Halfway to the tree, Joss had the sudden conviction that she could win. Thunderbird was powerful, but he wasn't as young as Mabel, and he was carrying a heavier load. The gelding was making an obvious effort, but the little mare was just getting started. Her dainty hooves barely touched the ground.

I'm going to win! thought Joss exultantly.

Yet in the next moment, she found herself pulling ever so slightly on the reins, slowing Mabel down, letting Thunderbird fly past them and reach the sycamore tree a few seconds ahead.

Simon had won. And Joss had let him. She wasn't sure why. Not because of some dumb outdated code that said "always let the boy win." Truly not, although she imagined that Mabel was looking at her with large brown eyes filled with feminist reproach.

She had simply wanted Simon to win because she loved him. She wanted Simon to have such a good time that he'd want to see her again, which, when you came right down to it, was probably nothing more than that dumb and out-dated "always let the boy win."

Joss sighed. Sometimes it was hard to stay liberated.

But Simon was grinning all over his face, and the smile was so beautiful it made up for the temporary loss of Joss's independence.

Touching the tree, he leaped from the saddle and reached up to pull Joss down. For the space of a second or two, she found herself in his arms, and it was everything she had imagined, but then her feet touched the ground and he stood back and let her go.

"Let's sit awhile, okay?" he asked.

Simon took the horses' reins and looped them around

the tree trunk while Joss Marshall tried to find a spot under the tree that wasn't full of stones. No easy task in Connecticut. But at last she'd managed to brush away the biggest and sharpest of the rocks, and boy and girl sat down gingerly side by side.

Above their heads, the sunlight filtered through the branches of the tree. The leaves had all changed color, and many of them had already been borne away by the wind, but a few still clung to the tips of the branches, dried golden and brown.

For a minute or two they said nothing, while Joss was nervously certain that Simon would hear the beating of her heart in the silence and know instantly how she was feeling.

Then, of course, they both spoke at once.

"You first." Joss smiled.

"No, you," said Simon with a definite shake of his gorgeous head.

"I was just asking how you learned to ride so well in Connecticut."

A bold eyebrow shot up, and he gave her a lopsided smile. "Wyoming doesn't have an exclusive on horses," he reminded her dryly.

Me and my big mouth, she thought. Now I've insulted him. He thinks I'm patronizing and a snob. Joss wished she'd never asked the question.

But Simon was grinning again. "I've been around horses all my life, just like you. Matter of fact, some day I'd like to raise them."

"And I'm going to treat them. I want to be a vet," answered Joss enthusiastically.

"That so?" The handsome eyebrow went up again. His eyelashes were impossibly long and thick, especially for a boy. "Well, then, ma'am, I'll bring all my horses to you for doctorin', even if I have to round 'em up in Connecticut and take 'em down the Chisholm Trail to Wyoming. On Highway One, of course.''

They both exploded into laughter at the thought of a roundup and a trail ride in the 1980s, and after that, things grew easier between them and they sat together, talking comfortably, until the position of the sun in the west told Joss what she didn't want to know.

"Oh," she said sorrowfully, looking at her watch. "I have barely enough time to get back to the stable. I'm going to have to leave right now."

They scrambled to their feet. Simon looked a little embarrassed.

"Jessica, do you mind if I don't ride back with you? I'd like to give Thunderbird a good run. He needs the exercise."

His words struck Joss like a blow. Naturally, she had assumed that Simon was enjoying her company as much as she was enjoying his and that he'd want them to be together until the last possible moment, as she did. But apparently that was not the case.

"Of course I don't mind," she said stiffly, hoping he wouldn't hear the hurt in her voice.

"But, listen, can I ask you something? Do you think you'll be riding next Saturday afternoon?"

"I might," she said, trying to sound casual, struggling against the sudden bright flair of hope.

"Well, could we make that a definite date, do you suppose? Could we meet here at, say, one-thirty, at this tree? I sort of think of it as *our* tree, unless you think that's too dumb."

A beatific smile spread over Joss's lovely features. "I'd love to. And no, I don't think it's dumb. Not at all."

She turned to climb into the saddle, but Simon stopped her. "Jessica," he murmured softly.

And then she was in his arms, and he was kissing her hard, holding her against him. Instinctively, Joss's arms tightened around his neck and her eyes closed as she gave herself up to his kiss. It was like no other kiss she had ever received. She wanted it never to end.

But it had to end, and she had to ride back to the stables. If she were to return to Holly Hills late, she might be grounded and there would *be* no next Saturday, no date with Simon under the tree. *Their* tree.

Joss had never been so happy in her entire life. She wanted to dance in the saddle, to jump up and down, but that would have been unfair to poor little Mabel. Instead she hugged the precious knowledge to her.

She was in love! Jessica Marshall was in love with Simon Slattery! She was going to see him again in a week! They had "their" tree!

Just wait until she told the other Jessicas!

CHAPTER NINE

Darryl

To Jessie Brown's delighted surprise and relief, Alex Edwards *did* phone and ask to see her again. There was a loud celebration in the Tower when she came back from the telephone breathless and happy, stardust in her large gray eyes. Jody yelled out, "Way to go, Jessie," and Joss gave her a big hug. As usual, little Jessica only let her smiling eyes do the talking for her.

Their first "date" was not to be exactly a date at all; Alex asked if he could call on her at the dorm. Joss had callers all the time, but Jessie had never sat downstairs on one of the lounge sofas where everybody could see her, trying to make conversation with a virtual stranger. She wasn't sure she could bring it off.

"Of *course* you can, you goof!" Joss laughed. "He's probably going to be just as nervous as you are. And besides, you're wrong if you think anybody in the Goldfish Bowl will be looking at *you*. All the other girls will be too wrapped up in their own dates to care about yours."

"Besides, it's fun to see just how far you can go and how much you can get away with," chimed in Jody, who had already had two parlor dates with the mischievous Grady Ferguson, and who had managed to sneak in a little hand-holding and even a tiny kiss or two, no more than a peck, right under the noses of the teacher on duty. On doctor's orders, Jody Rudolph was still forbidden to leave the school grounds, at least until the knee cast came off.

An hour before Alex was due to arrive, Jessie Brown lay down on the floor of the Tower and wriggled, at her room-mates' urging and with their clamorous encouragement, into the French jeans.

"I'm going to need at least a month to break these in," she moaned, struggling to her feet. "How's it going to look when I try to stand up to say good night to him, and I can't get my behind out of the chair?"

"Who said anything about a chair?" scoffed Jody. "Grab a sofa, or you two are never going to make any progress!"

And, although Jessie blushed at the idea of it, when the time came and her caller arrived she actually did find herself leading Alex Edwards to a sofa. And the jeans had relaxed enough for her to sit down next to him without making a total idiot of herself.

Alex was even better looking than she remembered, because that first evening out had been such a blur. Tall and thin, with a serious face but a sweet smile, thick, straight brown hair, and beautiful dark eyes behind aviator-framed prescription glasses, Alexander Edwards looked a year or two older than his real age of seventeen. He was properly dressed in his school blazer and tie, neatly pressed gray flannels, and newly shined shoes. A completely presentable person. Not exciting perhaps, but attractive in his own calm way. Which just suited Jessie, who had never craved excitement.

It was just as Joss had promised. After a quick once-over to check out the boy one of "the four Jessicas" had snagged for herself, the other girls in the Bowl turned all their attention to their own dates, and Jessie and Alex were left on their own.

Their conversation was odd, at first. Jessie's Down East

clipped way of speaking contrasted strongly with his lazy Virginia drawl. More than once, they had to ask each other "What? What was that you said?"

Once, when Jessie had asked Alex to say a certain word a second time and it had proved to be nothing more than the word *dog*, she'd laughed. "That's a one-syllable word."

"Honey"—he grinned, exaggerating his southern speech—"Wheah Ah come from, theah *are* no one-syllable words."

After that, the ice was broken, and soon it melted away entirely, and Jessie felt completely at ease.

They were alike in many ways, both of them serious students with strong motivations and fixed career goals. Jessie's future world was science, Alex's law. His father was a prominent attorney in Lynchburg, with his eyes on the state senate and, perhaps later, on Washington. Alex seemed determined to follow in the family footsteps.

Strangely enough, their home situations were mirror images.

"Have you got brothers and sisters?" she asked him.

Alex cast his eyes up to heaven and sighed. "No brothers. All the sisters in creation. Three older and two younger. And me the only boy."

"You're making that up!" shrieked Jessie.

"Would that I were." Alex sighed. "But why would I ever want to make up such a scandalous lie?"

"Because you're teasing me, and because somebody told you that I'm the only girl in my family, and that I have three older brothers and two younger."

"You're not serious!"

"Would that I weren't!"

Amid laughter, the anecdotes flew thick and fast between them. Jessie's having to play shortstop to fill out a baseball team, Alex being compelled to take dancing lessons and escort his dateless sisters to local cotillions.

"I never thought I'd met a girl who understood what I had to go through. Especially such a beauty as your sweet li'l self." He smiled.

"Why, thank you, sir," replied Jessie, batting her eyes and pretending to fan herself. She never in her wildest dreams would have believed that she'd be doing a Scarlett O'Hara impression to amuse a boy she really liked!

The evening was over too soon; curfew had to be obeyed and the boys back at their own schools in time, or they wouldn't be allowed back to Holly Hills for weeks.

"Gentlemen, it's time to go home, now," called Mrs. Hayward firmly, coming into the Bowl.

Alex rose instantly to his feet and held his hand out courteously to Jessie, to help her up. Southern manners, drilled into him by one mother and five sisters. But Jessie accepted gratefully, still insecure about the jeans.

"I surely did have a good time, Miss Jessie," he drawled, exaggerating again to make her laugh. "May I dare to hope that this evening might be repeated in the very near future?"

"I do declare, sir, I'd be honored."

"What about this Saturday night? Is it one of your date nights? Would you like to drive into Kenton and see a movie?"

"It is and I'd love to."

"Great! I'll phone you tomorrow, but hold Saturday night open for us."

Us. He didn't say *me,* he said *us.*

Jessie's heart danced all the way up three flights of stairs to the Tower, and she came into the room grinning so broadly that Jody immediately cracked, "Uh-oh, she's got it bad. It's a full-on case of the loves. Somebody take her temperature, quick!"

"Oh, for heaven's sake, Jody Rudolph, grow up! He's

just a nice boy and I like him. Don't go making it into something it isn't."

"*Yet,*" added Jody wickedly. "Well, here we are. I can't get rid of Grady, Jessie appears to have snared Alex, and Joss is riding the range with some mysterious stranger. The only one left is you, little Jessica, and we're going to have to do something about that real soon."

Jessica Prud'homme de la Reaux squeaked in terror and hid herself under her blanket.

"Really, Jody!" Jessie Brown was genuinely annoyed. "At least leave the child alone. You know how that kind of talk always upsets her."

"Child! She's sixteen if she's a day!" protested Jody.

"Fourteen," came a little voice muffled by blankets.

The other three turned in shock, staring at the bed. "Fourteen and a sophomore?" gasped Jessica Marshall in disbelief.

"Well, almost fifteen. I'll be fifteen October twenty-fifth. I guess I just had good tutors . . ." The girl's face was pink with embarrassment.

Immediately, Jody Rudolph hopped to little Jessica's bed and sat down on it to apologize. "I'm sorry if I said anything to hurt your feelings, little one. Sometimes I forget how rough I can get. It's all that competitiveness they pounded into me, and now it has no athletic outlet."

"No, please, it's all right. I *want* to grow up, truly I do. But everybody in my life has always kept me such a baby— my father, the servants, my governesses, my tutors. The nuns at the last two schools I went to. They've always surrounded me, protected me, and sheltered me. I've never been permitted to make my own decisions, and I'm not sure I'll ever be able to. Maybe I'll never learn to stand on my own two feet."

"Of course you will! We'll all help, won't we, Jessicas?"

"Yes!"

"Okay," said Jody. "We'll make that a top priority. Jessica Prud'homme de la Reaux will be standing on her own two feet by the end of the semester!"

Jessie's Saturday night date with Alex came off smoothly. That was the word for it . . . *smooth*. Compared with the rough-and-tumble manners she was used to with her brothers, Alexander Edwards' manners were as smooth as cream. But somehow, this time it left Jessie with a brand-new feeling: frustration.

She'd never wanted a boy to kiss her before. She'd never even thought about boys in those terms. But her feeling for Alex was different. It was too new and strange to be called *love*. Unlike Joss, Jessie was cautious in everything, and that included putting a name to her emotions.

But, nameless or not, Jessie Brown had to admit she had emotions of some kind about Alex, and those feelings included wanting to be kissed. Maybe it was only curiosity, maybe it was "the natural blossoming of biological urges," as her mother had once put it to her in one of their mother-daughter chats, but whatever it was, it was starting to drive Jessica Brown crazy.

If only Alexander Edwards wasn't such a damn gentleman!

She'd seen him only twice, but it was enough for her to know that he was attracted to her, and yet so far he hadn't laid a glove on her. Not even a finger of a glove.

What was a girl supposed to do? Jessie found it impossible to confide in Joss. Joss could never have encountered such a problem in her own social life. She always had to peel boys off her body like old Band-Aids.

Jody wasn't the kind of girl you could tell this to, or before you knew it she would have organized a committee and made it "a priority" and Alex would be coerced into kissing Jessie whether he wanted to or not. Jody Rudolph would have taken the decision right out of his hands.

So, oddly enough, Jessie Brown took her dilemma to the least likely person in the world who could solve it, fourteen-year-old Jessica Prud'homme de la Reaux, who still slept with a teddy bear.

"He respects you, that is obvious," murmured Jessica.

"That's the problem, all right. How long is it going to take him to respect me less or want me more?"

"Why not ask yourself why you have so little patience so suddenly?"

Jessie looked startled and stared openmouthed at the younger girl. "You're pretty smart for fourteen," she said at last.

"Juliet was fourteen," pointed out Jessica Prud'homme de la Reaux. "Perhaps if she'd been sixteen or seventeen she and Romeo might have lived. What I'm saying is that events possess a natural rhythm of their own. Force them, and perhaps they will not come to the proper end result. You do not know what may be going on in Alex's mind or heart. His struggle may be even greater than yours. It is very difficult to overcome all those years of influence and upbringing."

Jessie regarded little Jessica with awe. Imagine that giant brain in that tiny head! The three of them had never paid enough attention to her or given her the proper credit for her vast intelligence. She was absolutely right. If Jessie allowed everything to proceed in its own time at its own pace, then she would know when it was right, and so would Alex.

"Thanks, Jessica. Your advice is going to fit my head as well as those designer jeans fit my behind, and I thank you again for both."

But the next time that Jessie Brown was called to the telephone it was not Alex Edwards. It was a boy she didn't know at all, whose name she had never heard before, who identified himself as Darryl. Darryl Croft, from Foxleigh School.

"I'm a friend of your brother's," he said in his deep and thrilling voice. More a man's voice than a boy's.

"Which brother?"

"Randy. Met him at summer camp last year, we were both junior counselors. He told me he had a sister at Holly Hills. I've been meaning to phone you, but I flunked intermediate algebra, and I've been putting in extra hours to catch up. Just passed the retake exam, and I'm a free man. Want to go out and celebrate?"

"I know just how you feel. Intermediate algebra is flail time for me too. If one of my roommates wasn't such a math genius, I'd be up the same creek without the same paddle."

"So how about going out with me, and we can define the elusive binomial theorem together."

For an instant Jessie hesitated and then she thought, Why not? She wasn't going steady or anything, and this boy sounded like what Jody would call "real kill." *Why not?*

"Saturday night?"

Well, Alex hadn't asked her yet, and maybe this would goad him to a little action. Nothing like a spark of jealousy to set fire to a boy's britches. "Sure. That'll be fine."

"Can you meet me somewhere?"

"Meet you? No, that's out of the question. Haven't you ever dated a Holly Hills girl? We can't ever go out without the boy picking us up and showing a pass from his school. Don't you know that? They must have the same rules at Foxleigh that they have everywhere else."

"Uh, sure. I forgot. It's been so long since I've been out, thanks to algebra. Yeah, I'll come get you at seven. Do you think you can be ready and waiting down in the lobby for me? Um, that way we'll have a longer time together. And I really hate to be kept waiting; makes me nervous.''

Maybe this Darryl was some kind of flake, and Jessie had been too hasty. She didn't remember Randy ever mentioning a Darryl Croft. Was it too late to back out now? On the other hand, Randy never talked to her much about anything. They mostly shot baskets together, one on one. And you only live once. She took a deep breath, and then a chance.

"I'll be ready," she promised.

At seven on the dot on Saturday night, a tall boy swept into the downstairs lobby and presented a pass to Mrs. Hayward. Jessie had been sitting downstairs for five minutes, trying to decide whether she was doing the right thing or whether she was in need of a frontal lobotomy. She had tried several times to get her brother on the phone, to check this Darryl out, but Randy had not returned any of her calls.

But blind dates with "a friend of your brother's" were common practice among the girls she knew, and on first inspection the boy appeared to be almost human, even if he didn't have a head or a face.

A long Foxleigh muffler in the school colors of green and gold was wrapped several times around his neck, covering his chin. A woolen nerd cap was pulled down over his hair and his eyes were hidden by glasses with Coke-bottle bottoms for lenses.

It was going to be a boring evening, thought Jessie as he grabbed her hand and hustled her out of the lobby. Well, it served her right.

But once in the silver Honda he had waiting outside, Darryl threw off the cap and unwound the muffler and took off the glasses and looked Jessica up and down with great appreciation.

"Your brother should be shot first and then hung. All he

said was 'skinny sister'; the word *ravishing* never left his lips. Face it, Jessica, you're a beauty and Randy is a retard.''

Jessie gasped. She was looking into the single most beautiful masculine face she had ever seen in her life. This Darryl Croft was what Jody would call ''a fox.'' No, correction. ''A humpy fox,'' the highest praise Jody Rudolph could award. Darryl was worth every syllable of it.

''Where to?'' Turning the key in the ignition, he grinned at her.

''I . . . I . . . don't know.''

''Music? Movie? Dancing? Dinner? Any or all of it, gorgeous Jessica. *You* decide.''

She closed her eyes and went for broke. ''All of it.'' Then she added hastily, ''But I have to be back no later than eleven or I'm grounded.''

''We'll have to see what we can do, then. Buckle your seat belt. We're off.''

There was a roadside disco about ten miles from Holly Hills, and it was always packed on a Saturday night, with long lines of boys and girls waiting to get in. Darryl threw the guy at the door a twenty-dollar bill, and the next thing Jessie knew they were out on the floor, boogieing to the Police. Darryl was the best dancer she'd ever danced with, moving smoothly to the music, making her look good.

They'd danced for about fifteen minutes when Darryl grabbed her hand. ''Had enough?''

Actually, Jessica hadn't had enough, but she was in no mood to argue, she was so in awe of this dazzling boy. ''Sure.''

''Okay, food next, then a movie, if you still want to go.''

''Food'' turned out to be a little Italian café just on the outskirts of Kenton, where Darryl ordered a fantastic meal

—antipasto with fresh shrimp and little crisp rings of fried squid—*calamari*. Having been raised in a coastal town, Jessica didn't blink an eye at the squid, but dug right in. The antipasto was followed by large bowls of spaghetti with tomato and basil sauce, which was followed by veal and mushrooms which was followed by Jessie yelling "Stop! I can't eat another bite!" just as the little plates of spumoni ice cream were put down in front of them on the red-checkered tablecloth.

"That's it for me, I'll explode in a minute," she groaned. Darryl reached over and grabbed her dessert, polishing it off right after he finished his own.

Where did he put it? Apart from his extraordinary broad shoulders, he was very slim, with no hips, lean flanks, and a flat belly. Yet he could eat like an army. This pleased Jessie; it reminded her of home, of how her brothers could tear into their food as though the Russians were invading before dessert.

By the time Darryl Croft had finished an espresso coffee and paid the bill, there was only an hour left before curfew, and a twenty-five-mile drive back to Holly Hills. There went the film, but Jessie didn't mind. She'd had a wonderful time, basking in this beautiful boy's frank admiration of her.

Over dinner he'd praised her hair, her figure, and did everything but write poems to her eyes. It was obvious that he was taken with her, and it would be almost impossible not to fall for him. His charm was equal to his looks, and his smile was a killer. He was the most exciting person she had ever encountered; and it was almost a miracle that he was interested in her! Plain old Jessie Brown! *Un*-bee-*lee*-va-bul!

She hadn't thought about Alex Edwards all evening, but she thought of him now, comparing the two boys—one so calm, the other so exciting—as they went speeding back to Holly Hills. And they *were* speeding, doing sixty-five instead of the legal forty miles an hour on this road. Why was Darryl in such a hurry to get her back? They'd have a full half hour to spare before curfew. Was he bored with her already?

How could she have been no naive, she wondered as his mouth crushed down on hers. They were parked outside the school gates; and as soon as Darryl took the key from the ignition, he pulled Jessie into his arms. And kissed her, and kissed her, and kissed her. And there wasn't a thing she could do about it but kiss him back.

The only time that Jessie Brown had ever been kissed by a boy was when her name had been called in the childish game of Post Office. At the age of eleven, she had entered the dark little room with her stomach churning, only to face Artie Keegan, a boy she went to Sunday school with, a boy as nervous as she was.

Artie had grabbed her quickly and pressed a kiss on her mouth, his lips shut tight. He was wearing braces, and Jessie's lips had ached for two days.

Darryl's kisses were nothing like Artie's. They were hot and demanding, and she trembled under them, crying "no, no," but not really meaning it. When he placed his burning lips against her throat, he put one hand on her breast, and she tried to pull back, but failed. She felt his hand fondling her, and it seemed as though her own flesh was betraying her, rising eagerly to meet his fingertips.

This was not the Jessie Brown she had been all her life; this was a different person altogether, a person who responded to Darryl Croft's kisses with a warmth almost equal to his own.

"Beautiful," he murmured into her throat. "Beautiful, beautiful Jessica." Then his lips covered hers again.

"I . . . I . . . have to get back," she gasped weakly.

Darryl looked at the digital clock on the dashboard. Five minutes to eleven.

"Yes, you do," he said reluctantly. "I don't want you grounded, beautiful Jessica. I want to see you and see you, and see you . . . But you'd better go before I change my mind and grab you again. If I do, I don't think I'm strong enough to let go." Kissing her lightly on the lips, he opened the door and let her out. "I'll call you. Sleep well. Dream of me."

Jessica's legs had turned to rubber, and her heart was pounding; she could barely make it up the driveway. She had to run the last few feet to get checked in by eleven.

Jessie was so exhilarated from the events of the evening that she completely forgot the question that had been nagging at the back of her brain all evening. What had become of those thick glasses Darryl had taken off and never put back on again? Oh, well, it wasn't that important. Maybe he wore contacts. So many people did.

"Dream of me," he'd said when he'd kissed her good night.

As though Jessica Brown had any choice.

CHAPTER TEN

Big Macs and Fries

The following morning, when the other three asked her how her date with Darryl had gone, all Jessie could mumble was "fine."

"Where did you go? What did you do?" they wanted to know.

I went to heaven and I fell in love, she thought. But out loud, all she could say was, "Nothing special. We danced for a few minutes at Farnum's and we had dinner at an Italian place."

"Is Darryl good looking? Is he nice or is he nothing? Are you going to see him again?"

How could she explain the perfection of his face and body, the passion that he had awakened for the first time? Jessie could only shrug, but little Jessica Prud'homme de la Reaux, with her sad, wise eyes, looked underneath the shrug to the confusion and insecurity that lay beneath.

Later, when they were alone, Jessica asked Jessie softly, "Do you want to talk about it?"

"No! Yes . . . I'm not sure. Oh, Jessica, remember what you said about events having their own natural rhythms? Well, last night was an event that was just too fast for me! I couldn't keep up with it! And now I'm so mixed up I'm not sure what to do or what to even think!"

"What do you feel?" the younger girl asked. "Feeling is, I believe, sometimes more important than thinking or doing."

Jessie bit her lip and tossed her long braid impatiently. "I'm not even sure of what I feel. I never fantasized about a boy like Darryl. He's so exciting, so mature, so . . . hard to handle. But now that I've been out with him, Alex seems so dull! To tell you the truth, I think I'm in love with Darryl, but I'm scared to death of it! I was better off not knowing him! Oh, Jessica," she burst out, "I *want* him!"

"*La coeur a ses raisons qui la raison ne connait pas,*" murmured Jessica.

"The heart has its reasons . . ." translated Jessie slowly, "which . . . which . . . ."

"Which reason itself knows nothing of."

"Well, it sounds terrific in French, but it doesn't do me any good. What am I supposed to do?"

"Do nothing," advised Jessica. "If you are not presently in control of your own life, make no important decisions. Try to drift with the tide for a little while and see in what directions it takes you."

"You mean go on seeing Alex and Darryl at the same time, if both of them call me for dates. Which I doubt," Jessie added gloomily.

"If that's the tide. Perhaps you won't have to make up your mind. Perhaps events will make them up for you."

"And perhaps I wish I'd never heard of hot rollers or French designer jeans!"

"Perhaps"—little Jessica smiled—"but I doubt it."

"Okay, the name of the game is Gross-out. Is everybody clear on the rules? The point is to tell us something true about your family, about any member of your family, that is so gross and so sordid that the game stops. We keep going in rounds until we give up. Whoever stops the game cold wins. But it has to be true," added Jody Rudolph. "We used to play this after workouts, and it was really kill. Joss, you go first."

"Why me first?"

"Why not?"

"Okay." The four girls were sitting around on their beds in pajamas, their homework assignments completed with still a few minutes to go before lights out. Jessie was painting Joss's toenails with siren-red nail polish when Jody came up with the idea of the game.

"Come on, come on."

"You have to give me time to think," Joss complained, knitting her pretty brows. "I don't come from a very large family, and the Marshalls are not gross. But anyway, here goes. I have two eleven-year-old cousins, a girl and a boy, and they're twins. And you know what their mother named them?"

"No, what?" they all yelled together.

"Donny and Marie!"

Everybody groaned in disgust, but Jody called out, "Not bad, Marshall, for a beginner, but no cigar. Jessie, you're next. You've got brothers, so this is bound to be really repulsive."

"Well," Jessie began slowly, "I never told anybody this, but this is about my mother, not my brothers. She wears T-shirts that say 'Women Hold Up Half the Sky' or 'The Cock May Crow, but the Hen Delivers the Goods.' "

"Wears them in *public*?" whispered a shocked Joss.

"To the supermarket," Jessie wearily nodded.

"That's okay," Jody judged, "but not a game stopper. I'll go next. When my mother was pregnant with me, she went to the Woodstock Music Festival, barefoot, wearing only a tie-dyed minidress and flowers in her hair. And she told me that she almost named me Rainbow Star-World."

An awed silence fell on the group, then Joss made gagging sounds while Jessie wrinkled her nose in disgust and whispered, "I think we have a winner."

Little Jessica Prud'homme de la Reaux murmured

sarcastically, "Thank you for sharing that with us."

"Yeah, that one always cops the prize." Jody laughed. "I guess you missed your turn," she said to Jessica.

The youngest girl shrugged. "I have virtually no family anyway. No mother, no brothers or sisters. Just my father, and Monsieur Leroi."

"Is that the guy who calls you up every day for a report?"

"Yes, my father's aide-de-camp. I see much more of him than I ever do of Papa." Despite herself, Jessica sighed heavily.

"It must have been very lonely without a mother," Joss said gently. "Do you want to tell us about it?"

Jessica shrugged sadly. "All childhoods are the same, I think. If you are rich, you think everybody in the world must be rich. If you are poor, then it's natural to be poor. If you grow up alone, you think others are alone as well. I had a friend whose parents were divorced when she was a baby, and she was always surprised whenever she learned that somebody had a father at home. She found that most unusual."

"Was it interesting being a diplomatic brat?" Jody wanted to know.

Jessica put her head to one side and considered the question. "Interesting? *Odd* would perhaps be a better word. For example, when my father was stationed in the Far East, we lived in the diplomatic compound, behind a high stone wall. All the embassies were close together, like houses on a street. We Western children were never allowed out of the compound; we had to play only with one another, whether we were friends or not.

"But the oddest thing was that we were not permitted to walk, even to the next embassy. We had to be driven there in the official car. So you would see these giant black automobiles, Rolls Royces, Daimlers, moving slowly around the compound, from one house to the next, delivering children to play together. When I think about the way things are in America, I find that odd. At the time, though, it seemed very natural to me."

"Did you go to diplomatic balls and receptions?" asked Joss in a hushed tone.

"Once or twice." Little Jessica nodded. "From the outside, they appear to be very glamorous and exciting. But actually they are as boring as a shoe dealers' convention. Because that's all anybody talks—business. Only the business happens to be diplomacy instead of shoes, and the ladies wear elaborate gowns and jewels instead of polyester pant suits and badges."

"You must have been very lonely, growing up with only servants and tutors," said Jessie thoughtfully. "And Monsieur Leroi." She thought of her own large, close, noisy family and shuddered in sympathy.

"Yes, it was often lonely. But I have met lots of lonely people who are surrounded by loved ones. One doesn't have to be alone to be lonely. And I have always had my books, my beloved friends. Books were always my best friends . . . until now." And she smiled shyly.

"That's true," said Jessie. "Believe it or not, being the only girl in a family of boys can get mighty lonely. There are things you can't really say to brothers, or to any boy, for that matter. And my mother had her hands full with six of us, so she didn't often have much time just for me."

"I was an only child," put in Joss. "And I can tell you it gets lonely in Wyoming, especially in the winter when you're cut off from the world. If I didn't have my beautiful Moonlight Sonata, I'd have gone nuts sometimes."

"And thank heaven for Brandy." Jessie smiled, thinking fondly of her golden retriever. "I could tell Brandy everything."

"I always had a cat." Jessica Prud'homme de la Reaux smiled. "A little cat to curl up beside me while I read, or sleep on my pillow with her paw in my hand. I miss Mitzi very much; I wish I could have a cat here. But sometimes Mrs. Henderson the cook lets me stay in the kitchen for an hour and hold her Orlando on my lap."

"I never had a cat or a dog, never had the time," said Jody Rudolph suddenly and abruptly. "Nobody ever gave a damn whether I was lonely or not."

This was very unlike Jody. For one thing she was always cheerful and optimistic, never allowing a bitter edge to her tone or words. For another, she was usually silent as the grave on the subject of her days as a gymnast. But now her friends sensed that she might be ready to open up a little.

"Were you lonely?" whispered little Jessica.

"About as lonely as a girl can be. All anybody ever seemed to care about was my scores, not about *me* as a person. Was I getting too tall? Putting on too much weight? Was my floor routine good enough to impress the judges? Could I hold on to my competitive edge? Never: 'Jessica, what are you thinking or feeling? Jessica, do you want to talk about something?' It was always, 'Jessica, let's try that again. I think you can do better this time.' It was always 'Jessica, be the best,' never 'Jessica, be yourself.'

"From the time I was five years old I lived in practice clothes. I can't remember wearing a dress more than four times in ten years. My coach was my father and mother, my trainer was my sister and brothers. I can't tell you the title of the last book I read, it was so long ago. Where would I find the time to read? I'd fall into bed at night so exhausted I'd be asleep before my head hit the pillow.

"The worst thing was, I didn't have friends, I had competitors. Oh, they were friendly, and good sports, and cooperative and all that 'team spirit' jive, but they'd all keep their eyes tightly on you whenever you were on the bars or on the mat, to see if they could spot a weakness. I know, because I did the same thing myself.

"All we ever cared about was winning. Winning big. Going for the gold. That goddamned gold! All my life I trained for it and worked for it and did without Big Macs and fries and drive-in movies and friendship and love, and for what? I never even got near the gold and now I never will!"

Her curly red head bowed, and tears flowed down her freckled cheeks as deep sobs racked her body.

The other three crowded around Jody, hugging her, wiping her eyes, holding her tightly, making her part of themselves.

"Well, you've got friends now. *And* love!" cried Joss.

Sympathetic tears formed in little Jessica's dark eyes. "And Big Macs and fries too!" she wept, breaking everybody up.

Jody sat up and blew her nose, and the tears turned to occasional sniffles. After a moment, her familiar freckle-faced grin broke out. "It wasn't all bad," she assured her friends. "I really enjoyed competing. I really enjoyed being the best, when I *was* the best. Being up there on those bars, knowing that you're good, that your moves are perfect, *feeling* it with your entire body . . . well, there's no thrill in the world quite like it."

She turned her face to look at her three friends. "But I've learned something, Jessicas. And I've learned it from you all, and I'm grateful for it. I've learned that competing isn't all there is to life. It's going to take me awhile, though, and you're going to have to be patient with me. I know I still come on like Miss Champion Athlete, but I think that's because I haven't yet found anything to take its place. Competition is addicting, it's hard to do without once you've had a taste of it."

"So are Big Macs and fries," squeaked Jessica Prud'homme de la Reaux.

CHAPTER ELEVEN

Problems

When the first trimester's grades were posted, all four of the Jessicas were on the Dean's List of the sophomore class. Jody Rudolph's system had paid off. Their study/tutorial hours had given to each of them the help she needed in her weakest classes—Jody in history and English, Jessica in math, Joss in French, and Jessie in sociology. Miss Appleyard was very pleased with them, and said so publicly. The word shot around the school like a brushfire.

The Apple was happy with the four Jessicas! Their names were on everybody's lips; the four Jessicas, they were on their way to becoming a school legend. The celebrated quartet went almost everywhere together, arm in arm. They'd even taken to dressing, if not alike, then similarly. Tight jeans, loose sweaters. The same ugly but comfortable shoes that Jessica Rudolph had to wear for her injured knee were adopted proudly by the other three. Jody had kept the ribbon on her cast, so each of the four Jessicas proudly tied a different color ribbon around her own right knee. Jody's was red, Jessica's blue, Joss's green, and Jessie's a bright buttercup yellow. They had become a clique, a closed society. The rest of the school envied them.

The Apple was particularly proud of the progress that little Jessica Prud'homme de la Reaux had made. A timid mouse when she'd first arrived, a girl who wept at night from loneliness, she was now able to speak up in class, smile at other girls in the school and return their greetings, and had even managed to get herself elected to the Shakespeare Society, an extracurricular group that devoted a couple of hours every week to exploring the more difficult works of the Bard.

Membership in the Shakespeare Society was restricted to only the most promising literature students, although everybody wanted to belong. This was because the society was allowed to go on field trips to Boston and even New York to see professional productions of Shakespeare's plays. Not only that, but the field trips were co-ed. There were chapters of the society in just about every New England prep school, and the boys and girls were allowed to sit next to one another at the plays and even grab a bite together before the buses left.

Many a romance had begun on these trips. Wasn't it worth agonizing over *Pericles, Prince of Tyre* or *Timon of Athens* to get the chance to see a New York play and eat a New York pizza with some new boy? But the society was very selective; to be asked to join was quite an honor, and the three Jessicas were so proud of the fourth that they planned a little surprise party in her honor. Besides, it was soon to be her fifteenth birthday; they hadn't forgotten.

To the outside world, it appeared that Jessica Prud'homme de la Reaux was the baby mascot of their group. In reality, the situation was very different. Although the youngest of them, Jessica was also in many ways the wisest. Being so isolated over the years had given her a chance to develop a mind that was almost free of trivialities—she could cut right to the heart of any problem and pinpoint the solution.

Jessie and Joss found themselves often coming to little Jessica to confide in her, to ventilate their problems. And they both had the same problem: boys. Although Jessica Prud'homme de la Reaux had no experience at all with boys, she loved her roommates and wanted them only to be happy. She was troubled for both of them, Joss in particular, because Joss was so deeply—but unhappily—in love.

The Saturday after she met Simon Slattery, Joss Marshall was at the sycamore tree by one o'clock, her heart pounding, her hands icy yet sweating. Mabel's reins were looped around the trunk, the horse was grazing happily around the roots of the old tree. More leaves had fallen; the tree was almost bare, and a chill wind blew through the branches. Shivering, Joss pulled up the collar of her thin jacket and stamped her feet to get them warm, wishing she had worn gloves. She looked at her watch. Ten after one. Simon wasn't coming. She'd been a fool to ever think he was serious or that he'd keep their date.

A great sense of loss, more chilling than the wind around her, made her blue eyes fill with tears. What if she never saw him again?

But just at that moment, she heard the galloping hooves. There he was, riding toward her like a knightly hero out of an Arthurian legend—tall, straight, handsome. The arrogant tilt to his head made the pulse at her throat beat faster. He was grinning with pleasure as he saw her, and he waved one arm over his head. Smiling with all her heart, Joss waved back.

Simon reined in and literally threw himself out of Thunderbird's saddle. He spoke only four words: "I'm late. I'm sorry," before he seized Joss tightly in his arms.

"Whoa!" she started to say. She never got the chance. His lips were on hers, and her mind went blank, filling up again with only one word . . . Simon, Simon, Simon.

How they went from a standing position to a horizontal

one, Joss would never know. One minute, they were pressed together tightly, Joss's back against the trunk of their tree, Simon's tongue pushing its way between her lips. The next minute, there seemed to be a blanket beneath her and Simon above her. Somewhere in her brain a little voice told her to say something, do something, before it was too late. It was already too late. Simon's ardent hands had worked down the zipper of her jeans while his kisses had intensified. His weight was crushing her.

She heard his voice, breathing harshly into her ear, "I love you, Jessica. Please let me, I love you."

"No, I can't!" she cried out. "Please don't ask me to do that!" But his physical strength was more than she could handle. His body wasn't asking hers; it was telling her what to do.

Now he was gently kissing her eyelids, kissing away her tears. "Are you okay?"

"I . . . I think so . . . I feel dizzy."

Simon cradled her in his arms. "Shhh. Just lie quiet for a minute." He stroked her soft golden hair.

Joss's teeth began to chatter.

"Hey, you're cold!" Simon stood up and stripped off his fleece-lined poplin jacket, wrapping it tightly around Joss. "That better?"

She nodded, still unable to speak. Simon tucked the blanket around her legs and sat down next to her, wrapping his long arms around Joss to warm her further.

"I didn't know . . ." he began awkwardly. "I mean, I never thought it would be your first time, a girl as beautiful as you."

Joss turned her face away from him, unsure of what to say, her face red with shame. Was she blaming him or herself? And was *blame* the right word for what she was feeling?

Simon buried his face in her neck. "Then I'm glad it was

me," he murmured. "Won't you look at me? Please? I won't bite, I promise."

Despite herself, Joss laughed. She began to think more clearly. It wasn't the end of the world, after all. She was still in one piece . . . almost . . . and the boy sitting here with his arms enfolding her was still the beautiful Simon, who was still telling her how much he cared.

She turned to look at him. His eyes were a darker blue than she'd seen before, dark with the intensity of his gaze. Putting two fingers under her chin, Simon tipped Joss's face up so that it was level with his. Then he laid his forehead against hers, then the tip of his nose against the tip of hers, then his lips met Joss's in the sweetest, softest kiss of her life.

"Hey, I'm sorry if I was rough with you," he whispered, kissing her again gently. "I didn't mean to hurt you. It doesn't have to be that way, you know." And their lips met again, this time lingering, reluctant to part.

The next Saturday it rained. Simon phoned.

"Can't you meet me somewhere?"

"Oh, Simon, I wish I could! But I can't just get out on a Saturday afternoon. It has to be riding, otherwise I have no valid pass! The only thing I can think of is if you could pay me a 'call-on' visit. I'd have to register you in advance, because you're not from one of the local prep schools, and we couldn't *go* anywhere. We'd just be able to sit downstairs and talk. We couldn't even hold hands! But it's better than nothing."

"Sorry, baby, that's an out. I work nights, didn't I tell you? Saving up for college. What are you saying, that if we don't ride, we can't meet? *Ever?* What if it goes on raining? What are we gonna do when it starts getting real cold?"

"Oh, Simon don't say that! I can't bear it!"

But Joss knew it was true. Soon it *would* be too cold to

ride. What would they do? What would she do if she couldn't see Simon? Already she ached for him, ached almost unbearably.

"Look, I gotta go," he said hastily. "Somebody wants to use the phone. Just pray for sunshine next week, and try to think of some way to squeeze out of that girl's jail you're locked into. If I don't see you soon, I'm gonna explode!"

"Me too," replied Joss fervently.

"Love ya."

"Me too."

Since that time, they'd seen each other only on three occasions, and each time they'd made love with hunger. Now, the end of October was almost on them, and every week brought shorter days and colder afternoons. Soon they wouldn't be able to meet anymore on riding days.

On the second afternoon of their three, Simon had pulled out a pocket knife. "I know this is totally geek, but I'm going to carve our initials on our tree," he told Joss.

"No, don't!" She jumped to her feet and grabbed his hand.

"Hey, why not? You ashamed of me?"

"It's a living thing! It's *our* tree, but it's also itself! How can you want to hurt it, to cut into its skin?"

He looked at her oddly, with an expression she'd never seen before and couldn't read. "You're right," he said quietly, folding the knife and putting it into his pocket.

The following Saturday as Joss rode up to the leafless sycamore, she couldn't believe her eyes! All over the tree were initials—"S.S." and "J.M." There must have been hundreds of letters, all made out of felt and pressed on. And there was Simon, grinning at her.

"They didn't hurt a bit," he told her proudly.

"This must have taken you hours to do!" she gasped.

"I came early," he said, "for a change." And he gathered the delighted girl into his arms.

That was the last time Joss had seen him.

Joss was getting desperate. Needing to talk to someone, she thought of Jessie first, but Jessie was very distant these days, not talking very much to anybody. She appeared to be wrapped up in some problem of her own, something she couldn't confide. It didn't seem to be the right time to talk to her about the irresistible Simon Slattery. So Joss brought her problem to little Jessica.

Jessica listened in silence as Joss poured out her heart.

"It is true love?" she asked at last.

"I think so," answered Joss uncertainly. "I'm almost sure of it. All I think about is Simon. All I want to do is to be with him and have him take me in his arms. It's too late for me to back out. I don't even want to back out. All I want to do is find some way to go on seeing him!"

"It would seem to be difficult, indeed," answered Jessica thoughtfully. "He works nights, you say? Even Friday and Saturday nights? He has never asked you out for either of those nights?"

"No," confessed Joss miserably. "No, we've never had a real date . . . just the meetings under our tree."

Jessica considered this for a moment. "Do you suppose," she asked Joss gently, "do you suppose there could be another girl, somebody he *is* seeing on the weekends?"

"Don't you think that suspicion hasn't occurred to me?" cried Joss bitterly. "I've asked myself the very same question at least a thousand times. But he's told me he loves me, over and over. Oh, God! What if he's lying? I feel like such a fool!"

And throwing herself into Jessica Prud'homme de la Reaux's sympathetic arms, Jessica Marshall broke into a storm of sorrowful weeping.

* * *

Jessica Brown was so torn up inside she didn't know what to do. Ever since her first date with Darryl Croft she had walked around in a daze, not knowing whether she was coming or going. All she did was stick close to the phone in the hall, in case Darryl should phone. The next time that Alex Edwards called her for a Saturday night date, she turned him down with a lame excuse, certain that Darryl would be calling.

But he hadn't called her. Not that week or the next. Finally, convinced she'd been put back on the shelf, she accepted a date with Alex. As though he'd been waiting for that as his cue, Darryl phoned.

"Is this the beautiful Jessica?"

She tried to keep her tone light, even though her pulse was hammering in her ears. "No, this is Jessica Brown. You want Jessica Marshall."

"Ah, but you're wrong," his thrilling voice lilted in her ear. "It's Jessica Brown I want. And want. And want. What are you doing Saturday night?"

Her heart sank to her shoes. "I already have a date," she said quietly.

"Break it."

Break it! Jessie was a girl who was raised to speak only the truth, never to deceive or dissemble. Ethics and morality had been drilled into her for keeps, by parents whose sense of values were rock-certain. She'd never told a lie in her life or broken a promise, and now this gorgeous boy with turquoise eyes was urging her to lie to and let down Alex Edwards, a decent boy whose only fault was that he wasn't Darryl Croft.

She broke the date. It destroyed her to do it, but the power that Darryl exerted over her was too strong for her to break. Jessie had never had feelings like these before. She simply didn't know how to handle them.

Here was the most desirable boy she'd ever met, and he was calling her beautiful! His kisses burned on her lips, his hands burned on her body, and it took every ounce of strength she possessed, both physical and spiritual, to keep him from going any further. She had trouble enough in the front seat of his Honda, but at least she'd never allowed him to persuade her into getting into the back-seat.

But Jessie Brown was still Jessie Brown, and she recognized that she was in the wrong, and that her feelings were leading her astray. She knew that Alex Edwards, with his quiet southern manners and his acute intelligence, was worth at least two Darryl Crofts, maybe more. She realized that she was hurting Alex, that he was genuinely fond of her and she was treating him shabbily.

Not to mention the risk she was taking. There was always the strong possibility that Alex might not wait for her to get over this infatuation and would let himself be snapped up by some other girl with more sense. She could lose him forever. And all because of a "love" that was probably no more than a strong physical attraction.

But she couldn't help herself. Whenever Darryl called, Jessie went running. Hating herself, but running. And one more time, Alex was the one who was left behind.

She wanted desperately to talk to Joss, her first and best friend at Holly Hills. Joss would understand, she would know what kind of magnetism turquoise eyes and broad shoulders and a cleft in the chin could exert on a girl of sixteen. But Joss seemed to be carrying such a burden of unhappiness of her own. There had to be someone she could talk to. She couldn't keep Darryl Croft to herself for one more minute.

She sought out Jessica Prud'homme de la Reaux.

"He hasn't made any committment?" asked Jessica.

Jessie shook her head mournfully. "No. He hasn't even

told me he loves me. All he says is that I'm beautiful and that he wants me."

"And . . . er . . . have you . . . ?" Jessica broke the question off at the point of delicacy.

"No, we haven't, honest!" cried Jessie, her cheeks burning. "Not that I don't want to. But the thought of it terrifies me! I'm just so confused! I hate lying to Alex, but I don't want to hurt him."

"And you don't want to give him up either?" prompted little Jessica.

"I can't." Jessie sighed. "I just can't. I don't know why, but I seem to be attached to *him* too. Only not quite in the same way. The thing is, the two of us are so much alike, and we have so many things in common to talk about. We enjoy the same books, the same music. It's comfortable being with Alex. Not exciting, but comfortable. I know it's unfair to Alex, but I don't want to lose that."

"And there's no chance of your giving up Darryl?"

"Never! Unless . . . he gives me up, which seems to be more likely. He doesn't even call me every week, just whenever he seems to feel like it. All I think about is being with him, kissing him. Oh, Jessica, you have no idea what it's like, being in love!"

"No, that is true," said Jessica Prud'homme de la Reaux quietly, and, to herself, she added, *Grace à Dieu*. *Thank God.*

CHAPTER TWELVE

Declaration of Independence

On October twenty-fifth, Jessica Prud'homme de la Reaux turned fifteen. First thing in the morning, she was handed a telegram of congratulations from her father and a little parcel that had arrived yesterday in America by diplomatic pouch. The box turned out to contain a string of pearls.

"Are those *real*?" breathed Jody, awed, as the three others passed the lovely strand from hand to hand.

"No doubt." Jessica shrugged. "It would never occur to my father to send me anything less. Or anything interesting," she added a little bitterly.

"Oh, and we've been *handling* them," cried Joss, hastily giving them back.

"No, handling pearls is good for them," little Jessica assured them. "They have to be worn frequently, or they die."

"Pearls *die*?" breathed Jessie.

"Yes, unless they are worn next to the skin, they lose their luster and they simply . . . die. They need human contact."

"Just like people," said Joss quietly. Jessica nodded agreement.

"*Oui*. Just like people. I suppose I had better sleep in them." She slipped the strand over her head, and it nestled at her throat, gleaming softly.

"Whew! Feature sleeping in pearls! That's full on!" Jody grinned.

For a couple of weeks now, the others had been planning a small surprise party for Jessica's birthday, just among themselves. Joss had taken a snapshot of the four of them to a photography place and had it blown up to life-size, bigger than a poster. Smuggling it back in hadn't been easy, but now it was safely hidden in Mrs. Hayward's room.

Jessie had been detailed to head Jessica off after her last class until everything was ready in the Tower and produce her at four-thirty P.M. on the dot. Mrs. Hayward, in conference with Miss Appleyard, had agreed to a few refreshments, as long as the party didn't get noisy or out of hand.

Jody was responsible for getting the birthday cake, with Grady Ferguson's help. St. Trinity was eighteen miles nearer Kenton than Holly Hills, and he'd bicycled over to the bakery and supervised the color of the icing and the "Happy Birthday, Jessica" written across the top.

"As long as I don't have to deal with the last name—Prune Danish Deli-Rooney," he'd informed Jody.

"Dork head." She'd rapped him affectionately in the mouth, and he winced. Jody Rudolph didn't know her own strength.

Last night, Grady had paid a call, with the cake, which was handed in surreptitiously to Mrs. Hayward. They were almost ready.

While Jessie went off to delay Jessica, the others set to work, decorating the Tower in red, white, and blue crepe paper festoons—across the ceiling and down the walls. Bunches of balloons of red, white, and blue were blown up with a mighty effort on Jody's part and floated from Jessica's bedposts. Even Jessica's teddy bear was wearing a triple bow of red, white, and blue, not only for the Stars and Stripes, but for the tricolor of the French flag, as well.

Then Joss struggled up the stairs from Mrs. Hayward's room with the huge photo blowup, which was placed against the far wall. The Tower was ready, and it looked sensational.

Promptly at four-thirty, Jessie marched up the stairs with Jessica, talking at the top of her lungs so the others would be warned. Joss ran to the curtains and pulled them shut, while Jody snapped off the overhead light, plunging the room into darkness.

The door opened. Jody and Joss stifled their giggles.

"But it is so dark!" protested little Jessica.

"Taa DAA!" cried Jody, snapping on the light.

"Surprise!" yelled everybody. "Happy Birthday, Jessica!"

She stood in the doorway, astonished, barely taking in the scene—her friends laughing and beckoning to her, the room resplendent in red, white, and blue—and all of it for *her*! They had gone to all this trouble for *her*!

Tears started in Jessica Prud'homme de la Reaux's eyes.

"If you cry," warned Jody, "I'll cream you!"

"If you *don't* cry," warned Jessie, "*I'll* cream you!" And they all took turns hugging her.

"This is the best birthday I ever had!" declared Jessica. "Even the one in Moscow, with all the caviar, doesn't compare to this!"

"You had a birthday in *Moscow*?" demanded Joss, stunned.

"My twelfth. It wasn't all that much fun. The evening was nice, though, we went to the Bolshoi and saw the ballet, and the huge chandelier was all lit up. They don't light it all the time, you know, only for special visitors."

"Let me get this straight," Jody said slowly. "They lit the chandelier at the Bolshoi Ballet just for your birthday?"

"For me! Good heavens, no! What could make you even think such a thing? Premier Andropov was present at the same performance, and they lit it for *him*! I just happened to be there. But it was beautiful anyway."

Jessica looked around the room. "Yet it was not as beautiful as this," she said softly. "Not all the chandeliers in all the theaters in the world are as bright or as beautiful as the Tower is today. Thank you, girls, thank you from the bottom of my heart."

Outside, the telephone rang, and all four girls jumped.

"Jessica Prud'homme de la Reaux, telephone," called a girl's voice from the hall. It was five o'clock. Time for the daily report.

The small girl squared her shoulders. "Come with me, all of you," she said with surprising authority, and marched off to answer the hall telephone.

The other three Jessicas crowded around to hear.

"Hello, Monsieur Leroi," she said quietly into the receiver. "Thank you, yes, I am enjoying my birthday. What did I do today? I made mud pies in the morning, baked them in the afternoon, decorated them with worms, and now I'm going to eat them."

A barrage of puzzled French poured out of the telephone. Jessica didn't bat an eye.

"I have a message for you to give to my father," she said firmly. "It is this. I shall be happy to tell him anything he wants to know about me, but only if he calls me himself. I'm fifteen now, and it's time I stopped dealing with middlemen. No offense, of course, M. Leroi. I wish you a pleasant evening, or, as they say in this country, 'have a good one, whatever.' "

And she hung up the phone.

"Way to go!" hollered Jody. "That was *some* bump'n declaration of independence!"

"*Faaan*-tastic!" Joss laughed, and Jessie gave her a slap on the back.

"Welcome to the world of growing up!"

With Jody hobbling in the lead, they brought the newly emancipated birthday girl in triumph up the stairs for her birthday cake and presents.

All three of them had chipped in to buy Jessica something special, a boxed set of the complete Greek tragedies in English. It was a pleasure to see her face as she unwrapped it, the words of gratitude sticking in her throat. But her hands, as she turned the pages, were so happy and so gentle that no words could equal them.

"There's a lifetime of happiness here," she whispered at last. "I don't know how to say thank you."

"I think you just said it." Jessie smiled.

"Before we proceed with the festivities," announced Joss importantly, "I have something for each of us. A trifle, a mere nothing, don't everybody crowd me at once. I have a fish for each of you seals. Here, catch!"

From a shopping bag she took out four parcels and, glancing at the labels, distributed them, one to each, including herself.

"Don't line up to thank me, girls. Just send a check or money order; we also accept MasterCard and Visa. And we have an eight-hundred number for you to call."

"What is it?" asked Jessie.

"Try opening it, maybe that will tell you something, doo-doo-head," answered Joss affectionately.

"No! Everybody at the same time! On the count of three! One, two, three!" and Jody ripped open the paper.

T-shirts, all of them bright red. On the back of each "The Four Jessicas" was emblazoned. On the front was a screen-print of the photo in the blowup, the four girls together and smiling. Under each photo was a name—"Joss," "Jessie," "Jody," "Jessica."

"Wow! Team jackets! Ruff!" Jody laughed.

"It's a wonderful idea! When did you find the time?" asked Jessie.

"The same place that did the blowup did the T-shirts. I'm in hock there until I graduate, but what the hell, we only live once. But you all have to promise never to wear them in public. Let's keep our nicknames to ourselves—at least 'til we're seniors."

Jody and Joss agreed at once. Little Jessica said nothing, but sat on her balloon-decked bed, stroking her T-shirt as though it were her beloved Mitzi-cat, obviously very moved.

Now it was time for the birthday cake, and with a lot of whispering and orders given and contradicted, the three of them finally managed to get it up the stairs in one piece, get the candles lit on the landing, turn off the lights and bring the cake in, brightened by fifteen candles and one to grow on.

"Haaappy birthday to youuuuuu," they sang, almost on key.

"We wanted to get sparklers, but the Apple said positively not," they said. "We couldn't decide between chocolate and vanilla, so we got both," they said. And, "Make a wish! Make a wish!" they said.

Jessica Prud'homme de la Reaux closed her eyes and bent forward, blowing with all her might, right, left, in the middle, until every candle was out. Then she sank back, winded but happy.

"You'll get your wish, but only if you don't tell us what it is," warned Joss.

"I think you all know, anyway." Jessica smiled. *I wish that we may all four remain best friends forever.*

Three days after Jessica's birthday party, the Shakespeare Society was informed that its request to visit New York to see an off-Broadway production of *Twelfth Night* had been granted. They were to leave Saturday afternoon at four, have dinner in Greenwich Village, see the play and be home, tucked safely into their respective beds, by midnight. Unless the bus broke down, which everybody prayed would happen.

This was Jessica's first field trip, and she was greatly excited. It was also her first school excursion of any kind without the other Jessicas, and she was nervous.

"Boy, I wish I were you," said Joss enviously. "I've never even been to New York, let alone to the theater, let alone with a boy."

"I'm not going with a boy." Jessica blushed. "I'm going with a whole group of Holly Hills Shakespeare snobs. Big, as you say, deal."

"*And* Shakespeare snobs from Chalfont and Cumberland Prep too. If you think you'll be sucking up spaghetti with Elvira Malone or Lisa Wagner, think again. The cards are going to be well shuffled before the hand is played." Jody laughed. "I guarantee you'll wind up sitting next to the king of hearts."

Jessica looked toward Jessie in alarm, but Jessie only smiled at her and nodded her head. She had a date with Darryl for Saturday night, and she was so happy she wanted little Jessica to be happy too.

But Jessie wasn't to enjoy her happiness long. The next evening, when the phone rang, it was for her, and Darryl was on the other end, smoothly breaking the date.

"Something important has come up," he was telling her earnestly while she held the receiver to her ear, stunned. "Beautiful Jessica, I would much rather see you, but this thing with my father . . . well, I can't get out of it. You understand, I'll make it up to you, baby. I'm sure you understand."

But all Jessie heard was his voice, so many weeks ago, saying "Break it," when she'd told him about her date with Alex. "Break it." So cold. Behind his smooth words, she had a sense of that coldness now, and she knew she was really in trouble.

Every sensible bone in Jessie's spare New England body was telling her that she was better off without him, but she was unable to listen. Darryl Croft was lying to her from the jump; this was the perfect opportunity to cut her losses, tell him to shove it, and get the hell out of the relationship. She couldn't do it. Boy, was she in trouble!

Stricken, Jessie hung up the phone and went off somewhere all by herself to cry alone. The only place she could find was the second-floor john, which was, fortunately, empty, at least for as long as it took her to weep in private.

"Listen," said Simon Slattery urgently over the phone. "I've *got* to see you, Jessica! I'm leaving town Saturday night, and I'm not sure when I'll be back, maybe a week or two, maybe never."

"Are you in trouble?" cried Joss, her heart in her mouth.

"Well, you could say that, but it's nothing I can talk about over the phone. Please get out Saturday afternoon; do it for me, can't you? Just this once?"

Just this once? Was he really going away, where she might never see him again? Was he in trouble with the law? Drugs? Theft? Not for the first time, Joss realized just how little she actually knew about Simon Slattery. Only enough to make me love him with all my heart, she thought.

"Jessica? Darling? You still there?"

"Yes, Simon, I'm here. I'm thinking. All right, I'll try. I'll take my bicycle. If I can make it, I'll be at the tree. If I'm not there by one-thirty, don't wait. It means I couldn't get out."

"Honey, baby, don't tell me 'couldn't.' You're my girl and I love you. You'll find a way."

She found a way. She just left the campus, without a pass, without permission. If she was caught, it could mean expulsion, and she didn't even have a story ready. There *was* no story; what could she say? That she'd felt like an illicit bike ride on a gloomy late October afternoon? That she was meeting a boy she knew nothing about, but with whom she was in love? That she was risking everything for him because he'd called her "his girl"?

She reached the tree at one-fifteen, and he was waiting for her, his face somber, his eyes dark navy in contrast to their customary greenish-blue. Without a word, he caught her up in his arms, kissing her so hard it hurt. But Joss pulled away from him to look into his face, searching for the truth.

"What's wrong? What trouble are you in? Are you really going away?"

Simon avoided her gaze. "No, I'm not. I only said that to get you here. Jessica, I'm going crazy without you, you've got to believe me! I can't sleep, I can't eat, my schoolwork is going to hell. I love you, damn it! Doesn't that mean anything to you?"

At his words, a dam broke inside her, and her emotions came pouring forth like tons of rushing water.

"Not *mean* anything to me! How can you even say that! Do you believe for one moment that I would have made love with you if it didn't mean anything to me? But what can we do? We're *children*! We're powerless! If I don't obey the rules of my school, they'll bounce my ass over thirty states right back into Wyoming! Would we be better off then? Simon, I love you. I don't know the first thing about love, yet I know enough to love you! But if I go sneaking out of Holly Hills I'm bound to get caught, and if I get caught, I'll get expelled. Besides, I'm not the sneaky type, believe it or not. At least, I wasn't until I met you.

"All I know is that you say you love me, but you have

never, never *once* called me up for a Friday or a Saturday
night date! We're not even subject to the same set of rules.
You go to public school; you can do whatever you want on
Saturday afternoons. I'm supposed to take all the risks
while you do all the moaning!

"Now you tell me you got me out here, scared half out
of my mind for you, just to tell me you can't live without
me! Well, forgive me if I tell you that you're going to have
to! Much as I want to, Simon Slattery, I respect myself too
much to go on like this. If you want to see me, then call on
me at my dorm. You know the procedure. Good-bye!"

Climbing on her bicycle, Joss rode off without looking
back, and cried all the way to Holly Hills.

Jessica Prud'homme de la Reaux had been to theaters all
over the world and seen plays in all of the six languages she
spoke, but she had never been as excited as the day she
climbed into the bus with the rest of the Shakespeare
Society of Holly Hills.

She was looking her best; the others had seen to that,
rummaging around in the famous under-the-bed suitcase
until they found exactly the right thing for her to wear, a
tissue-soft wool dress of dark red that contrasted
beautifully with the black of her eyes and hair, and the
pink luster of the pearls she wore around her neck day and
night.

She had even put on high heels and perfume, a little
mascara and some blusher, although she had drawn the
line at Jody's offer of metallic powder to comb through
her hair.

"If we were going in the Daimler-Benz, perhaps," she
said with a mischievous grin. "But, my dear, for a bus,
glitter is totally *outré*. But totally."

After an hour's drive through the darkening countryside, the bus entered the rather dismal outskirts of New

York City, and Jessica found her thoughts wandering. So much had happened this term, not only to her, but also to the other three Jessicas. She herself had declared her independence and had started the painful process of growing up. She hardly slept with her teddy anymore, only now and then.

Joss and Jessie were in love, and miserable, and Jody was in like, and quite happy about it.

Therefore it must be better to be in like than in love, Jessica's logical mind told her. At least, until you were old enough to handle it. There *was* true love; it did exist. Of that she was certain. One had only to look at her own papa. He had loved her beautiful mama so much that he'd never gotten over her death, never thought to remarry, although he was certainly young enough. He was one of the most handsome, most eligible men in Europe or Washington.

That's the kind of love I'll have some day, if God wills, she thought. And it's worth waiting for.

The bus crossed the Bronx and rattled over the Cross-Bronx Expressway, heading downtown on the F.D.R. Drive. It was six o'clock now, and dark. Above the roadway stood the apartment houses of the rich—East End Avenue, Sutton Place South, Tudor City, Turtle Bay, Kips Bay. Below them, the slums of the poor, vast and sprawling settlements of ugly red brick, federally funded. Such contrasts in this city, thought Jessica.

At Chinatown, the bus turned off the highway and began threading its way west through the crowded traffic, to Greenwich Village. Here, the convoluted streets had names, not numbers—Jane Street, Charlton, Bethune, Bank, Waverly Place, Greenwich Avenue. It pulled up outside a *trattoria*—a small Italian café—near the theater.

The buses from Chalfont and Cumberland Prep had already arrived, and about thirty boys were waiting eagerly on the sidewalk in front of the restaurant. When they saw the Holly Hill girls, they yelled out boisterous greetings.

"Here they come! Too little and too late!"

"Play your cards right, girlie! I can be had!"

Hardly what one would expect from members of the Shakespeare Society.

Smiling in amusement, Jessica slipped into her beaver coat and picked up her purse and gloves. This was going to be fun. A month ago, she would have undergone torture sooner than making this outing in the company of virtual strangers. But what a difference a few weeks and three good friends had made! She was ready to face the world!

She waited, rather like a movie queen, for every other girl to leave the bus. Not that she was playing star, but she felt a tiny bit insecure in her high heels and was in no hurry to encounter a group of boys. Let the other girls have them; she was here to see *Twelfth Night*.

When she reached the door of the bus, she hesitated. The steps were so high! Suddenly, as if from nowhere, a strong hand gripped her arm and guided her firmly down the steps safely to the sidewalk.

"You're Jessica Prud'homme de la Reaux, aren't you?" a deep and thrilling voice asked. She looked up, into the most handsome face she had ever seen.

"I never thought I was going to meet you; I'd almost given up," the vision was saying, the smile of an angel brightening his features.

"My name is Taylor Windrum, and I go to Cumberland Prep. Call me Tay."

CHAPTER THIRTEEN

Happy Halloween

"If music be the food of love, play on, give me excess of it . . ." began the Duke of Illyria as he pranced across the stage, holding a perfumed handkerchief to his nose. With him went his musicians and courtiers as well as the attention of almost every member of the Shakespeare Society. *Almost,* because all Jessica was conscious of was the incredible, fantastic, ineffable, broad-shouldered, blue-eyed presence of Taylor Windrum, sitting next to her in the darkened theater.

His very presence radiated a kind of warmth, as though his body temperature was a degree or two warmer than other people's. Or maybe it was Jessica himself, blushing in the dark. Not a word of the play, which she knew almost by heart, was getting through to her.

If there was any food of love, it wasn't music. It was a bowl of linguini with white clam sauce, which is what Tay had ordered for both of them in the little *trattoria* near the theater. Although she had never mentioned it to the other Jessicas, Jessica Prud'homme de la Reaux had dined in the company of dukes and princes, and once, at a large dinner reception, she'd been seated next to Mick Jagger, but never had any meal overwhelmed her as the bowl of pasta she shared with Tay.

He'd been looking forward to this meeting for weeks, months, he informed her. His father was well connected in Washington (although he moved quickly over that part, before she could ask him any specifics) and apparently knew *her* father, and they'd missed each other in Paris by only one day, and once in Venice by a few hours.

"But I've caught up with you at last," he told her with a brilliant smile, "and now that I have, I'm not in a hurry to let you go again."

What was a newly independent fifteen-year-old girl to say to that, when the handsomest boy in the world was reaching for her little hand? Jessica Prud'homme de la Reaux could speak six languages, but she couldn't say "no" to Tay Windrum in any of them.

He reached for her hand again now, in the cover of darkness, and gave it a squeeze, then kept it tightly in his own. Jessica had never held hands with a boy before. So simple an act, yet so incredibly complicated. Was her hand sweaty? she worried. Was she allowed to take it back if her nose itched? If she took it back, would Tay mistake the gesture for one of rejection? Safer to let her nose itch than run the risk of offending Tay.

What was it Jody had said? Something about the cards being shuffled and Jessica sitting next to the king of hearts. Prophetic Jody, she was more on the money than she knew!

Jessica forced herself to pay attention to the play, and the oddest thing happened. Of all the Swan of Avon's comedies, she appreciated *Twelfth Night* the most. She'd read it numerous times, in several languages, had seen it played all over the world, including the Old Vic and the Young Vic in London, but here, in the dark with Tay, she understood it for the first time!

Always, she had reveled in the magnificent language and the sharp satirical comedy, but the romance had escaped her. Orsino's love for Olivia, Olivia's for "Cesario," who was Viola in a boy's disguise, Viola's apparently hopeless love for Orsino—all of these passionate, tangled affairs had held little or no meaning for Jessica.

Until tonight.

Tonight, for the first time in her life, when she heard the lines, "make me a willow cabin at your gate, and call upon my soul within the house," and "she never told her love, but let concealment, like a worm i' th' bud, feed on her damask cheek . . . was this not love indeed?" Jessica felt tears stinging her eyes. Only the sure knowledge that it would all end happily—that Viola would win Orsino and Sebastian would marry Olivia—prevented her from actually bursting into tears.

What had come over her? Another line of Elizabethan poetry kept sounding in her head; she couldn't seem to shake it loose. Christopher Marlowe had written it first, but Shakespeare swiped it for *As You Like It:* "Who ever loved who loved not at first sight?"

Who ever loved who loved not at first sight?

No, impossible. She was distracted by Tay's good looks and unbelievable charm, "turned on," as Jody would no doubt say. But love? At first sight? That was for plays and poems, not people.

Love was what her father still felt for her mother. Yet, remembered Jessica, he'd met her when she was only sixteen and had fallen in love with her on the spot. Juliet was only fourteen when she fell in love with and married Romeo. But Juliet died of her love. Thoughts tumbled through Jessica's head as she watched the play, her hand clutched tightly in Tay's. Now, for the first time, she was suffering for the lovers up there on the stage, even though this was a comedy, and they were neither star-crossed nor doomed.

Were she and Taylor Windrum star-crossed?

When the lights went on for the intermission, Jessica

blinked in astonishment to find herself in a theater. She'd been so wrapped up in her own thoughts, in the problems of the four lovers, in the presence of Tay, that she had been taken completely out of herself and into another world.

"Wait here," ordered Tay briskly, "and don't move."

He ran up the aisle as Jessica watched in wonderment. She saw him stop another couple, talk to them earnestly, take something out of his pockets and hand it over, and come running back down the aisle. The entire transaction, whatever it was, had taken him less than two minutes.

"Come on," he commanded, grabbing Jessica by the hand. "Intermission."

They mingled with the other students in the lobby, making conversation about the performance, talking to the teachers in charge, until the little bell sounded, announcing the end of intermission. The theater lights blinked twice, summoning the audience back to its seats.

Tay and Jessica remained behind.

"I gave those kids our seat stubs and ten bucks to sit in our seats after the lights go out, so that our chaperons will think we're in the theater," Tay explained, grinning.

"But—" began the mystified Jessica.

"I want to be alone with you," he said. "Come on." And he grabbed her hand again and dragged her out of the lobby.

"Where are we going?"

"We can't go to a bar, 'cause we're too young. We can't sit in any of these parks around here, 'cause they're full of alkies and junkies. There's only one place we can go. Trust me."

He hurried her along in a westward direction. Soon she smelled the distinctive, heavy, and not unpleasant smell of a nearby river. The Hudson.

A long pier extended out on pilings, right over the river. It was obviously a spot for lovers. People sat along the pier in entwined couples. It was dark enough so that nobody could see anybody else's faces. Even with the others there, it held a measure of privacy.

In her high-heeled shoes, Jessica stumbled on the rough boards of the pier and would have fallen if Tay hadn't grabbed her in time.

"Take off your shoes . . . no, don't. This wood is a hundred years old and filled with splinters."

In one swift movement, he had snatched her up off the ground and was carrying her in his arms to the far end of the pier. Astonished, Jessica let him. The strength of his arms was so thrilling that she felt faint, and she let her head droop onto his shoulder.

When he sat her down on a piling, she felt the sharp pang of disappointment; what she wanted was for him to hold her in his arms forever.

"You're as light as air," he told her, laughing. "I'm not even winded."

"I'm so afraid that we're going to get into trouble," fretted Jessica, wondering what she would tell Papa if Holly Hills found out and requested her presence elsewhere.

"Hey, chill out! All the world loves a lover, remember?"

"Then all the world hasn't met Miss Appleyard, our headmistress," retorted Jessica a little sharply.

"Don't worry, I'll get you back to the theater in plenty of time. We'll be safe on our respective buses in no more than an hour."

An hour! Is that all the time she'd have with him?

As though he'd read her mind, Tay said quietly, "I wanted us to have this hour by ourselves."

He slipped one arm around her shoulder and hugged Jessica to him. Suddenly she knew with clarity that Tay was going to kiss her, and her heart almost stopped. As he brought his face closer to hers, little Jessica had a moment of panic.

I don't even know where the noses go! she thought. But the thought was blotted out by his kiss, as sweet and gentle as her cat's touch. And, suddenly, she knew where the noses went.

"You're special, Jessica Prud'homme de la Reaux," said Tay in a husky whisper. "I hope you know that."

They sat on the pier, looking at the lights reflected in the water, from the ships, from the high-rise apartment houses on the other bank of the Hudson, from the World Trade Center downtown. She could see the Empire State Building, its magnificent summit lit up in three colors—red, white, and green.

And he kissed her again, as tenderly and sweetly as before.

All the way back to Holly Hills on the bus, Jessica felt Tay's kiss upon her lips. Her head was in a whirl, his words mingled in her brain with the words of *Twelfth Night*. She wanted to build a willow cabin at Tay's gate, but she wasn't even sure she'd ever see him again. Her young heart ached, not only for herself but also for Jessie and Joss, whose problems she finally understood. For whatever else love might be, no matter how smoothly and happily it was going along, it was a trap. Love held you fast and didn't let you go.

And wasn't it Shakespeare who said, "The course of true love never did run smooth?" He seemed to have the answer to everything, that Elizabethan wise-ass.

When Lisa Wagner tried to talk to her about the play,

Jessica pleaded a headache and rested her throbbing temples against the coolness of the bus window. She didn't want to talk to anybody; all she wanted to do was keep her eyes shut and Tay's kiss on her lips until she reached the Tower.

"You're never gonna believe this! The cast comes off on Halloween!" yelled Jody happily, limping in from her doctor's visit.

"Great! That's wonderful! About time!" chorused her roommates.

"I'm gonna paint a witch's face on it and send it out trick or treating!" Jody laughed. "Let's have a party!"

"We just *had* a party, for Jessica's birthday," Joss reminded her. "No way is the Apple going to stand still for another one in less than a week."

"No," agreed Jessie, "but we really do have to celebrate this historic event. We can't let history go unrecorded."

"Say, I know!" Jody exclaimed. "One thing we've never done is go out together on a double, no, scratch that, *quadruple* date! Why don't we all get together on Saturday night? Let's go somewhere and bury the cane and the cast by the crossroads at midnight!"

The other three suddenly looked acutely uncomfortable, not one of them meeting anybody else's glance.

"Uhm, well . . ." stammered Joss.

"I don't know . . ." began Jessie, looking doubtful.

And little Jessica, her dark eyes as round and as large as dinner plates, just shook her head fearfully and said nothing.

"Oh, I get it." Jody laughed. "You haven't got dates. That's burnt. But you've all got quarters and healthy fingers for a push-button phone, haven't you? This is 1986, man, not 1956! Girls are allowed to call boys for dates. So get on the horn and rassle up some guys and we'll all go out for a boss time! I'll even go first, and call Grady."

"That's easy for you to say," retorted Jessie, her cheeks on fire. It never occurred to her that she might telephone Alex; only that she didn't dare to call up Darryl. If he were to reject her, turn her down, it would kill her, simply kill her! "You've got Grady Ferguson on a leash. You say 'jump!' and he asks 'how high?'"

"Yes, and I for one am getting pretty sick and tired of your locker-room mentality, and between-the-halves pep talks! If I'd wanted to room with a cheerleader, I could have stayed in Wisconsin!" yelled Joss suddenly. It wasn't really Jody she was yelling at; it was herself, her having allowed herself to become so physically and emotionally involved with Simon, who hadn't been in touch with her for days now. Jody was the nearest convenient outlet for Joss's negative feelings.

Jody Rudolph turned brick red with anger and embarrassment. "What happened to the four Jessicas all of a sudden?" she demanded. "You two sound like Tweedle-Dumb and Tweedle-Dumber! Mellow up, can't you? All I was suggesting was that we party, but if that's too heavy for you guys to handle, then the hell with you! Roll your damn uptightness real small and stick it where the moon don't shine!"

And grabbing up her cane, Jody stormed out of the room, too angry to limp.

"Now look what you did!" snarled Jessie at Joss.

"What *I* did? What about what *you* did? You're the one who trashed Jody about Grady!"

"And you said 'locker-room mentality'! Did you think that wasn't a low blow?"

"Damn both of you, you *and* Jody the Jock!" yelled Joss with tears in her eyes, running out of the room.

Jessie turned angrily on little Jessica, who hadn't said a single word so far.

"Don't you look at me with those big brown eyes of yours welling up with reproachful tears! None of this was my fault, and you know it!" Then she, too, was gone.

Jessica Prud'homme de la Reaux sat silent on her bed, tears of sorrow and pain rolling two by two down her pale cheeks. After a minute, she picked her teddy bear up and rocked him in her arms, but this was not a child's problem, and it didn't call for a child's solution. With a sigh, she put him back on the bed. Then, reaching under her pillow, Jessica took out her beloved red T-shirt, with the picture of the four smiling Jessicas on the front.

Putting it up to her face, she burst out crying as though her heart would break in two.

"Christmas is coming early this year!" shouted Grady Ferguson happily as he got off the telephone. "Jessica's cast is coming off!"

Douglas McVie looked over the top of the copy of *Omni* that he was reading and kept his voice casual. "So Santa's unwrapping the box and giving the good little boy Ms. Muscle for the holidays? How cute." But his interest was as keen as a hound's for a possum, and his brain was going at seventy miles an hour down a three-lane highway.

"Stuff it, McVie! You can be such a pain in the butt sometimes, I don't know how you live with yourself. I know *I* can't." Grady was really angry.

Douglas smiled angelically, and his eyes shone like a matching pair of turquoises set in silver. "My apologies, Grady m'boy, and humble ones they are too. I take it that you and the fallen warrior are a definite twosome? Forgive me if I spoke rashly or rudely. I can be unwise at times." He sighed dramatically. "It's the Irish side of me coming out; we Celts are enchanted by the moon."

Whenever Douglas McVie wanted to make his roommate laugh, he laid the old W. C. Fields act on as thick as marmalade. It never failed, and it worked this time too.

"You are *such* a geek." Ferguson grinned. "The men in the white coats with the butterfly net are going to catch up with you some day and check you into a rubber room."

Douglas cocked one arrogant eyebrow. "So you and your lady are stepping out castless to celebrate?" he suggested.

"Saturday night. She just asked me. *She* asked *me*! Ain't that ruff?"

" 'Ruff' is indeed the word. And, I presume, all the lesser Jessicas will be in fond attendance? It will be a large, coupled affair, hot to trot for bowling or another such elite activity? Pizza and Pepsi and Devil Dogs for eight? Right this way, sir . . ." And he pretended to lift a velvet rope.

"Get real, McVie. It's going to be just us, just the two of us, Jessica and me. I mean, the roommates are all right, if you like roommates. But I've been waiting for this moment ever since I met her, and I want it to be special."

"Where are you taking her?" asked Douglas softly.

Grady bit his lip. "That's the problem," he admitted. "I blew my allowance on music videotapes for the VCR. I'd love to take her out someplace really nice . . . La Rêve for dinner, maybe. She lost all that weight she put on after the accident, and she looks a mite thin. I'd love to fatten her up a little. But I'm tapped out, McVie. Bone dry." He looked hopefully at his roomie, hoping the hint was broad enough.

Broad enough to drive a sixteen-wheel rig through it.

"La Rêve it is, my best chum," said Douglas McVie quietly. "Just you and your Jessica." He pulled out his wallet, which was usually bulging with cash. Douglas's stockbroker father never gave him any "quality time," but he sent him fat checks on a weekly basis. "Will a hundred cover it? If you need more, just say the word," he told Grady, peeling off the bills.

Ferguson's eyes popped. "A hundred ought to . . . no, better make it a hundred and fifty, just in case. I've never eaten there, but I hear it's harsh expensive."

"And thirty, forty, fifty. There you are, have a good time, children. Raise a glass of Perrier in memory of me."

"I'll pay you back, Doug, I swear it! Not all at once, but I'll pay every cent back."

"Not a second thought. Don't let it drift into your tiny mind. Just put your freckled face on the pillow and dream of escargots in butter sauce."

"What the hell are esk-ar-goes?"

"Snails, m'boy, and they're a requirement for graduation. If you want to be a man, you have to order them."

"Arrrggghhh."

There had almost been a reconciliation among the four of them on October 31, when Jessica Rudolph returned from the orthopedist without her knee cast. Somehow all the others managed to be in the room when she came home to the Tower, like cats who want to show affection but have to be very cool about it. Except, of course, for little Jessica, who loved them all but idolized Jody. There was nothing cool about Jessica.

When Jody came through the door, Jessica had risen to her feet with a big smile on her face, ready to congratulate Jody and hug her. She took a step forward, but the heavy scowl on Jody's face was so intimidating, she sat right down again with a terrified thump.

The other two, who had been watching little Jessica for their own cue, saw the scowl and the small girl's disappointment, and they, too, turned away.

And yet, ironically, the scowl was not what any of them thought it was. This was the first time that Jody had climbed those stairs without the double support of the cane and the cast, and it was a frown of intense concentration, with fear behind it. If she had only seen Jessica taking that tentative step toward her, Jody would have flung her arms wide and all four would have had a good old cry and lots of hugs, kisses, apologies, congratulations.

But Jody, under physical and emotional strain, was at that moment unaware of her surroundings, unaware, too, that her brows were knitted together fiercely. When she had finally come in the door, she looked around, hoping for a kind and happy word from any one of her room-mates. All she wanted was to be friends again. She wanted to share this wonderful moment with the Jessicas.

But by that time it was too late. She saw little Jessica's face turned away. Joss and Jessie were sitting with their backs to her. The hurt of it cut into her so deeply that she walked in silence to her bed.

By Saturday night, the silence in the Tower was thick enough to be sliced and toasted. The four of them slouched around miserably, each one wanting to say she was sorry and to suggest making up, but none of them, not even little Jessica, wanted to be the first. They had hurt one another too badly.

The rest of the Holly Hills campus was abuzz with the news. The four Jessicas had split up! Oh, they were still rooming together, but they weren't talking. For one thing, their room, usually filled with laughter and chatter, was as silent as a Chaplin movie. For another, the four of them were no longer seen arm in arm, moving through the day with happy camaraderie.

Bad news carries quickly, and soon a distressed Miss Appleyard heard of the state of affairs in the Tower. What had been a healthy situation for all concerned now appeared to be a hurtful one, one that required that the Apple herself (she knew how her girls referred to her behind her back) intervene and perhaps break the foursome apart.

After the weekend, she'd have to call all the four Jessicas in, one by one, for a stiff interview and maybe even relocate them. As for the room they called the Tower, evidently she had made a mistake in allowing them to have it, a mistake she'd have to correct as quickly as she could.

On Saturday night, Jody was the only one with a date. Simon Slattery still hadn't telephoned Joss. Jessie hadn't heard word one from Darryl Croft. As for Taylor Windrum, he had apparently vanished from Jessica Prud'homme de la Reaux's life as quickly as he had entered it. It was a long-faced and sullen trio that watched Jody Rudolph getting ready to go out.

With the loss of the eight unwanted pounds, Jody looked exactly like her *Sports Illustrated* cover photo, lithe and spare. Her best silk dress fit her again, and she slipped it on over her head and smoothed it to her sides. The dress was of such a dark gray as to be almost black, and it clung to her slender flanks with a loving touch. Above the collar, her red hair shone like burnished copper.

You look absolutely beautiful, Jody, thought Jessie, but she said nothing.

Knock 'em dead, killer, thought Joss, but she said nothing.

I'd be so happy if you would wear my pearls with your lovely dress, thought little Jessica, but even she said nothing, although she ached to.

Sad and alone, Jody walked slowly down the stairs to meet Grady Ferguson.

Sad and alone, each of the girls in the Tower turned away from the others.

Some celebration!

CHAPTER FOURTEEN

La Rêve

La Rêve was the unfulfilled dream of almost every girl at Holly Hills. As the ritziest, most expensive restaurant within a seventy-mile radius, it was naturally the topic of much conversation in the private schools of the neighborhood. The consensus was: if a boy was really hot for you, he'd take you to La Rêve for dinner. It was the culinary equivalent of giving you his class ring, and it cost a lot more than the ring. Some Holly Hills girls had celebrated special occasions such as Dean's List or Sweet Sixteen at La Rêve with their parents, but as everybody knows, parents don't count. Nerds and turkeys didn't count either. You had to be taken there by the boy of your choice or you might as well eat at Burger King.

La Rêve was status. Grady Ferguson felt two inches taller as he escorted Jessica Rudolph in past the gas-lit carriage lanterns through the elegant front door.

McVie had impressed upon him the crucial importance of slipping a finif to the maître d'.

"You have to tip everybody except the busboy, and that means *everybody*—the doorman who lets you in, the maître d' who shows you to your table, the captain who hands you your menus and calls your waiter over, and your waiter. If you go to the john, it's a buck for the lavatory attendant. If *she* goes to the john, it's *two* bucks. On your way out, you tip the valet who parks your car and you tip the lady who checks your coats. Is that it?" He ran the list over in his mind. "I think we got 'em all."

"Ye gods!" yelled Grady, "how will we afford to eat?"

"Hey, you're the one who wanted to play restaurant hardball to impress Jessica the Jock. Don't go chicken on me now! You're actually getting off easy; if you weren't under the drinking age, you'd have to tip the wine steward too. I hope La Rêve doesn't have a soda sommelier just to serve Tab."

Now, as the maître d' smoothly pocketed Grady's five bucks, he smiled benignly at the young couple. "Reservations for two? Yes, Mr. Ferguson, we have your table ready. This way, please."

Grady sneaked a peek at Jody; impressed to the molars, she whispered back, "Radical!"

It would be worth every penny he was in hock to his roommate for if he could show his girl the time of her life. Especially after what she'd been through. The terrible accident, the loss of all her hopes . . . Every time he looked at her, a little piece more of him melted into mush.

She was so beautiful tonight, all dressed up for the occasion. Her copper hair was as glossy as the silk dress she was wearing, and she carried herself straight and tall, with only the merest suggestion of a limp. The freckles he hated on his own face he thought adorable on hers.

The maître d' seated them and snapped his fingers for the captain, who came over with the menus, just as Douglas had predicted.

"Something to drink?" asked the captain, but his eyes said "no."

"Um, I'll have a Tab, please, with some lemon and plenty of ice," ordered Jody. Score another goal for McVie.

They opened the huge leather-bound menus and Jody gasped, her eyes wide! So did Grady!

"The prices!" she squeaked.

"It's written in French!" he squeaked.

Douglas McVie had given him the short course. "Never, never, *never* attempt to order in French. You'll only make a dork of yourself and be a laughingstock in the kitchen. Just read the menu and order in English. 'I'll have the lamb chops, pink, please,' or 'Give me a green salad and the small steak, quite rare.' Then at least they know you can read French, and you don't have to hassle with the accent. Oh, and when you're old enough to order wine, do it this way: call over the wine steward, tell him what you'll be eating, and ask him for his suggestion. When he picks out a wine, think about it for a minute, frown, and shake your head 'no.' Then say 'yes' to his *second* suggestion, and you'll blow him away."

Grady remembered those words, but he had expected the menu to be a printed one, not hand-written in purple ink in that strange European penmanship that Americans find so illegible.

For a moment he was tempted to close his eyes and point. Instead he said as calmly as he could, "I'll have the lamb chops, pink, please," praying that there were lamb chops on the menu.

"An excellent choice, sir," approved the waiter. "And for mademoiselle?"

Jody gulped, still knocked out by the prices, which were all in double digits *before* the decimal point.

"If I may suggest . . ." said the waiter.

"Yes, please!" Jody sighed in relief.

"The lemon sole is lovely and fresh tonight, and we have chicken breasts sautéed in *beurre blanc avec champignons.* It's been very popular this evening."

"The chicken breasts," decided Jody, "light on the

beurre blanc and heavy on the *champignons*. I'm on a diet." Thanks to Jessica Prud'homme de la Reaux, her French accent was perfect. Grady was more knocked out by her than ever.

Thank God *that* ordeal was over! They sipped at their sodas and glanced around the room.

La Rêve had been originally built as an inn sometime in the mid-1700s, and the oldest part of the building was of stone, like so many houses in Connecticut. In the intervening centuries, the building had been enlarged and added to, in a helter-skelter kind of way, to create not just one large dining room but a series of smaller dining rooms opening one into the next.

Grady and Jody were seated in the prerevolutionary part of the inn, where a wood fire burning in a large stone fireplace made a cheerful blaze. The ceiling was low, built them to conserve heat, and there was a romantic coziness about the place that warmed them both. Grady picked up her hand and fondled it.

"Jessica, we've been seeing each other a lot this term, and you know I really . . . like . . . you." He blushed, his bashful lips unable to form the word *love*. "Well, what I'd like to ask you . . . I mean . . . uh . . . will you . . . ?"

"Yes?" Jody smiled, waiting impatiently for the punch line.

"Grady, m'boy, what a pleasant coincidence. So glad to bump into you!" called out a thrilling voice. "Are you having a good time? Won't you introduce me to your beautiful lady?"

Ferguson looked up, scowling. That sneaking smarmy slimy bastard, he thought. No wonder he was in such a hurry to lend me a hundred and fifty bucks. He's been hot to get his mitts on my Jessica ever since I started going with her.

But Grady was on the spot. McVie had him cornered in a

public place, an elegant and expensive public place, and he had no choice but to act civil. No less was expected of a Ferguson.

"Jessica Rudolph, this is my roommate, Douglas McVie."

And Jody, with a tiny gasp, looked up into the angelically smiling face of the most handsome boy she'd ever seen in her life.

"This, I can truly say, is an honor," purred Douglas. "I've been a fan of yours for lo, these many years. Why, I even keep a photograph of you on the back of my closet door. The cover you did for *Sports Illustrated.*"

Clenching his fists, Grady ground his teeth. The truth wasn't in that sonabitch! And there was Jessica, all dazzling smiles and flashing dimples, bowled over by that stupid cleft in Douglas McVie's chin, just like any of the dumb nits McVie made out with and threw over. Grady had thought better of Jessica. He couldn't believe she was superficial enough to fall for McVie's line of horse manure. Was this the girl he was in love with, the girl he had been on the very verge of asking to wear his class ring? I've been set up! he thought. And by a guy I thought was my best friend!

For now McVie, who must have had this up his sleeve from the jump, was sitting down at *their* table, actually pushing in between himself and Jessica, never taking his eyes off her.

McVie, summoning the wine steward over with an imperious snap of his fingers. McVie, calmly perusing the wine list, as though he weren't six months under the legal drinking age! If Ferguson had tried that, they'd have booted him out of his fancy joint ass over teakettle. But McVie had the wine steward calling him "monsieur" and sitting up and barking for dog yummies.

Jessica was looking as though she'd also be eating out of

McVie's hand in a minute. Her cheeks were pink and her eyes were sparkling, and she was laughing at McVie's line of patter while Grady's heart turned slowly but surely to a rock in the middle of his chest.

What if I got up from the table and just simply walked out of here? he wondered. Would they even notice that I was gone? I doubt it. I don't know what the hell to do. Should I stand my ground and try to face-off with the world's greatest make-out and bullshit artist, or should I let him fake me out totally and just fade away? And what about Jessica? Is she smiling at him to be polite because he's my roommate? If that's the case, then why is she leaning over like that? She hasn't looked at me once since McVie sat down.

It was, in fact, true. All of Jody Rudolph's attention was focused on Douglas McVie. Never had she laid eyes on anything so gorgeous. His smile, that cleft in his chin, the deep turquoise color of his eyes, the thick wavy hair, the impossible width of his shoulders—he was knockout city on the hoof. But what came out of his mouth would make the grass grow tall and bright green.

As undeniably attractive as Douglas was, Jody decided, he was an arrogant, self-absorbed fake-out! The nerve of him horning in on her and Grady, taking over as though he owned the place, pouring wine with easy charm. Why, he was even coming on to her, right under the nose of his date, who was, as it happened, not only his roommate but supposedly his best friend! This boy was some piece of work!

She could see how uncomfortable and even resentful Grady was. He had every right to be. Jody had just about decided to come out cold and tell this Douglas McVie that she and Grady would prefer to be alone when Mr. Wonderful said something that made her stop in her tracks.

He had been pouring sweet syrup all over Jody, telling her how lovely she was, when he put the cherry on top of the whipped cream.

"Even a girl as beautiful as Joss can't really hold a candle to you, Jody," he purred into her ear. "You have something so . . . so—"

Jody! He'd called her Jody! How on earth could he know that her nickname was Jody or that Jessica Marshall was called Joss? Their nicknames were strictly private among themselves—to the outside world they were always known as "Jessica," each and every one of them.

Even Grady didn't know that her roomies called her Jody; he always called her Jessica. And if Grady didn't know, how could Douglas McVie know? If none of the other Holly Hills girls were aware they had private names, who could have told him?

Only one person. Only one of the four Jessicas. But which one? Everything seemed to point to Joss Marshall herself.

But why? How?

Only if she was in love with him. Jody knew Joss pretty well by now. She was not one to break a promise, unless she was totally unaware that she was doing so.

But Joss had never mentioned Douglas McVie, and if she'd been going out with Grady Ferguson's roommate, surely Grady would have known about it. They could have double-dated. But Joss was staying home on Saturday nights, even though she was one of the prettiest girls in the school. The only boy she used to moon over and talk about was a Simon Slattery . . . and she didn't even mention *him* anymore . . .

Hold the phone! Simon Slattery . . . Jody racked her brains. Wasn't he tall and gorgeous, and didn't he have a cleft in his chin, and didn't Joss once mention privately to

Jody eyes like Indian turquoises . . . eyes exactly like the ones looking deeply into Jody's now?

She leaped to her feet. "Grady!" she barked. Grady snapped to like a private when the general gives an order.

"Grady, get the check and take me home!"

"But, Jody, we haven't had dessert—"

"*Now,* Grady!"

Jody turned to Douglas and smiled long and sweetly into those turquoise eyes. "I'm *so* sorry I have to go," she almost purred, "but the cast only came off this morning and I'm suddenly tired. You do understand?"

"Will I see you soon?" he whispered urgently into her ear. "I want to see you very soon. Alone, of course." Douglas glanced furtively at Grady, who was furiously emptying his wallet to pay the check, but who was still managing to catch the action going on between his *former* girlfriend and his *former* best friend.

"You certainly will hear from me," vowed Jody, echoing her words in her mind. *You bet your heinie you'll be hearing from me, buster!*

On the way back in the car, Jody and Grady said no more than two or three words to each other. Grady was so steamed by what he considered Jessica's betrayal that he couldn't bring himself to speak to her. Besides, the pain was so enormous he was afraid he'd disgrace himself by busting out crying!

As for Jody, her mind was racing with suspicions, and she couldn't share them even with Grady. It wasn't only Joss who was on her mind, it was also Jessie, who was so obviously unhappy. Not only that, even little Jessica Prud'homme de la Reaux had taken to crying in her bed at night again, just as she'd done at the beginning of the term when she had been so unhappy and lonely. What had happened to the four Jessicas? What had divided them and driven them apart? Why were three of them so miserable? Jody thought she'd just discovered the answer. The tall, handsome, turquoise-eyed answer.

Jody knew that Grady was hurt and angry, and she promised him silently that she would soon make it up to him a thousand times over, but a hurt and angry Grady was unfortunately exactly what she needed at this moment.

So the two of them didn't speak, and the dream evening at La Rêve turned into a nightmare.

The three Jessicas were sound asleep in their beds when Jody marched in and snapped on the lights.

"Wake up everybody. Now!" she ordered, her cheeks pink with excitement. "Rise and shine. I have a feeling the four Jessicas are in deep trouble, and I have a feeling I know the way out."

CHAPTER FIFTEEN

The Four Jessicas

At first, Jessica Marshall, Jessica Brown, and Jessica Prud'homme de la Reaux listened with angry, incredulous ears to Jessica Rudolph's suspicions. Yet as Jody's logic unfolded, their three hearts began to sink and unhappy conviction crept into their minds.

"Does he have a voice that sounds like Log Cabin being poured on a waffle?" asked Jessie glumly, remembering long and ardent telephone conversations with Darryl Croft.

"With melted butter," confirmed Jody.

"And you say his eyes are very large and very blue, *non*? And they turn up at the corners with long, long lashes? And his head tilts to one side as he looks at you, so?" Little Jessica's impression of Taylor Windrum was right on the money.

I still can't believe it! How is it possible? agonized Joss silently. He held me in his arms and told me he loved me! How could he have lied to me so? What made him do this to me? Her cheeks burned with guilty humiliation. As Joss's beloved memory of Simon Slattery shattered into a million fragments, so did her heart.

All the pieces suddenly fit, like a jigsaw puzzle coming together. For the first time, they saw the pattern. Saturday afternoons with Joss. Occasional Saturday evenings with Jessie. The one Saturday night date "Darryl" broke with Jessie, "Tay" turned up in Jessica's life. Once he'd hit on all three, once he'd broken three hearts, there was no reason for him not to come on with Jody under his own name. All he had to do was turn on the charm, swipe her away from Grady, and his triumph was complete; Douglas McVie would have destroyed all the four Jessicas. The boy was truly evil; gorgeous, but evil.

"I should have kept calling until I'd reached my brother Randy!" mourned Jessie. "Obviously there *was* no Darryl Croft."

"Not necessarily," pointed out Jody. "There might be some poor innocent jerk at St. Trinity or any of the other schools named Darryl Croft, whom your brother *does* know. I wouldn't put it past McVie to help himself to any identity that was useful. He's also smart enough to cover his tracks."

"And I should have asked him exactly who his father was and how he knew my father," said Jessica in self-reproach.

"And what if you had?" replied Jody. "He'd have had some plausible lie ready for you to swallow. You'd have been back where you started, staring into those big blue eyes."

Jessica's eyes began to fill, and her lower lip to quiver. The king of hearts—a deuce!

"I'm the dumbest one of all of you," said Joss in a low voice, while two spots of color burned in her cheeks. She kept her eyes down, ashamed to look her friends in the face. "For one thing, I fell the hardest and asked the fewest questions. Now I understand why I'd never seen Thunderbird in our stable. He was stabled at St. Trinity. Now I understand why he never asked me out for a Saturday night; he was busy with *you,* Jessie. Or why he never wanted to call on me here. He knew he'd be recognized, either by one of us or by any of the other Holly Hill girls he's dated."

Inside, though, she was in pieces, barely able to think. "Simon" held her in his arms and told her he loved her, not only once but many, many times. How could she tell any of the others this? Only little Jessica had been told the worst, and it was doubly humiliating now that Joss knew that Jessica had fallen for his line too.

Besides, in spite of everything, Joss realized to her horror that she was still in love with Simon, or Douglas, or whatever the hell his real name was.

"You were the only smart one, Jody, the only one who saw right through him," said Jessie.

"Don't give me too much credit. Those eyes were getting to *me*, too, and right in front of poor Grady, who was just getting ready to offer me his class ring, I think. I hope," added Jody, suddenly aware of how much she cared for that freckle-faced mischief.

"Let's face it, we were all pretty dumb, and we all got taken, although some more than others," continued Jody, not daring to look at poor Joss. "But what burns me is that he split us apart, he actually broke up the four Jessicas and made us the laughingstock of the campus. He's done enough damage already, but God only knows what he had planned for us. Why, we might have gone down as the four most idiotic sophomores in Holly Hills history! Brrr! We've had a narrow escape!"

The other three nodded somberly. The thought of a permanent escape from those beautiful blue eyes didn't hold all that much appeal.

"Okay," said Jody briskly. "The self-recrimination period is over. This is recess. No more torture. My motto is, don't get mad, get even. We'll clean that slime's clock for him."

"But how?" asked Jessie. "He's probably laughing up his sleeve at the four of us, and if the story gets around, which I'm sure is his intention, we won't be able to hold

our heads up, not only at Holly Hills, but with any prep
school in the east—girl's, boy's, or co-ed!''

"Yes, but the story isn't going to get around because it's
not over yet," Jody reassured her. "There's some un-
finished business between Mr. McVie and Ms. Rudolph,
because he assumes my tongue is still hanging out. Now
here's what I propose . . ."

And she told them her idea.

"Far out!" cried Jessie.

"That could work!" cried Joss.

Little Jessica Prud'homme de la Reaux picked up her
teddy bear and pretended to strangle it. *"Magnifique!"*
she said. *"C'est formidable!* We'll get that . . . how you
say . . . sleaze?''

"I'm sorry about the things I said to you, you know,
that locker-room mentality stuff. It was really dumb,"
said Joss in a low tone to Jody.

"And I'm sorry, too, for hurting your feelings," put in
Jessie.

"Me too," piped up little Jessica.

"No, please, we were all pretty stupid," said Jody. "If
only we'd trusted one another, confided in each other,
maybe Douglas McVie wouldn't have gotten to first base
with any of us. Besides, I owe you girls an apology too. I
shouldn't have always tried to run the show. You were
right, Joss, about my locker-room mentality. I haven't yet
come to terms with being unable to compete again, and it
makes me pretty obnoxious sometimes. You girls have
helped me a lot—an enormous amount—in my transition
to the real world, and I'd love it if you'd go on helping
me."

"Anything!"

"How?"

"Whatever you need!" they cried.

"Just go on being my friends." Jody sniffed. Her tears

were contagious. But after the crying and the hugging were over, determination set in.

"Who's gonna get McVie?" demanded Jody.

"*We* are!" chorused the three.

"And who are we?"

"The four Jessicas!"

"Say it again!"

"*The Four Jessicas!*"

"*I can't hear you! One more time!*"

"*THE FOUR JESSICAS!*"

CHAPTER SIXTEEN

Cleaning His Clock

"Hello, may I please speak to Douglas McVie? This is Jessica Rudolph. Thank you. Doug? Jody. How you doin'?"

"Jody, I was hoping to hear from you. I'm delighted. Can we get together?"

"You bet, that's exactly why I'm calling. I'd just love to see you again. And you did mention a possible date. As it happens, I'm free on Saturday night."

"Oh, some trouble with the freckle-faced Boy Wonder? Ferguson hasn't spoken a word to me since the other evening at La Rêve."

"Never mind about Grady," said Jody, making an enormous effort to keep her voice pleasant, even inviting. "How about *us*?"

"A fascinating question, indeed. Saturday night it is. Where shall we meet?"

"Meet? You mean, like on some street corner under a lamp post? Aren't you gonna pick me up here? We have a sign out, don't we? Holly Hills doesn't let sophomores just waltz out the front gate whenever the mood strikes them. It's easier to break out of a Nazi stalag than to get out of the school on Saturday night without a pass."

A strained silence answered her, then Douglas spoke too quickly. "Uh, I'm having trouble with my car, and I'm not sure if it'll be out of the shop by Saturday . . ."

"Well, I guess that's off then, sorry. So long, Doug—"

"No, wait! Give me a minute to think! I have it! Let me take you to dinner at La Rêve, we'll have a special evening. Uh, suppose I get somebody else to pick you up and sign you out and deliver you right to the restaurant door—"

"Like a pepperoni pizza?" demanded Jody, stifling her giggles. The rat was falling right into the trap. . . .

"Listen, I got a better idea," continued Little Ms. Innocent. "You know the boat house on the Holly Hills skating pond? I can sneak down to it if you can. Why don't we simply meet there? Nobody ever goes there at night, not at this time of the year. It'll be deserted . . . *our* place. Maybe you could bring a blanket and a little radio . . ."

"Radio? My sweet naive child, I own a laser disk player!"

"Swell, bring it. That way, nobody has to sign me in or out. I'll take the risk if you will."

"Jody, I'd ride through a ring of fire for you!"

Maybe you will, she thought. A ring of fire isn't such a bad idea, you slime. Out loud, she lowered her voice so that it oozed out into his ear. "We can be alone, Douglas. Just the two of us. Okay?"

"Better than okay; it's out of sight! Fan-*tas*-tic!"

"Can you make it, say, seven-thirty?"

"Count on it!"

"Oh, and Doug? In case I'm a few minutes late, you *will* wait for me, won't you? Sometimes it's a little hard to slip away with all those female eyes watching you . . ."

"I can get behind that, Jody. I'd never take my eyes off you myself if I could help it."

Butter and salt that corn and you could eat it raw, thought Jody. "All right, Saturday night at the boat house. Seven-thirty. I'm really looking forward to this, Dougie. With all my heart."

"Me too, gorgeous."

"Later."

Hanging up the phone, Jody made the "Okay" sign to the other three. It was set.

The week went quickly and the girls firmed up their plans. It was broken only by Miss Appleyard's sending for them, one at a time, for a private little discussion. It did the Apple's heart good to see that the girls were back together again and that they had formed an even stronger bond than before. Not only did each of them assure her that it was true, but they were arm in arm on the quad, for all of Holly Hills to see.

Before they knew it, it was Saturday night.

The boat house was, as Jody Rudolph had promised, deserted. It was also pitch dark and colder'n hell. Douglas McVie shifted uncomfortably on the wooden bench and pulled his jacket more tightly around him. Good thing they had a blanket. But he couldn't see his own hand in front of his face. Jessica should have told him to bring a candle or something. Well, next time he'd remember. But when the hell was she going to turn up? By now she was at least fifteen minutes late.

He heard a rustle in the nearby bushes and a light footstep.

"Jessica?" he called out in a near whisper.

"Yes," came the whisper back.

A slim figure slipped into the boathouse and slid onto the seat next to him. Immediately, Douglas McVie made a grab for it and kissed a fragrant girl full on the lips.

"Oh, Douglas," she murmured, pulling herself firmly away from his kiss. "You're wonderful, but I can't stay. 'Bye." And she was out the boathouse before a startled Douglas could get his bearings. Funny, she hadn't sounded like Jody at all; her voice was more like Jessie's.

Before he could collect his thoughts, she was back, her hands twined tightly—a little *too* tightly—in his hair. This time he grabbed her in the dark, and the kiss lasted longer and tasted different. No, this was definitely not Jessie. Could it be Jody?

"Jody?" he whispered, mystified.

"Call me Jessica," she whispered back. Then she too had vanished.

"What the hell is going on here?" called out Douglas McVie, starting to get nervous. He wasn't stupid, and something was definitely fishy here. Besides, he hated being teased, and was rarely subjected to it; girls were always dazzled by his phenomenal looks.

The door to the boat house slammed shut, and the lock clicked. Then he heard the sound of a wooden match striking, and suddenly the wick of a kerosene lantern burst into flame. The lantern, casting weird shadows on the ceiling, revealed four girls in matching red T-shirts. Four very angry girls. Four very angry girls named Jessica.

"Oh, shit," muttered Douglas McVie. "Trapped. Bummer."

"Ladies, allow me to present to you the lowest form of animal life, Mr. Douglas McVie of St. Trinity school," announced Jody Rudolph with murder in her eye.

"Oh, no, you're wrong!" cried Joss Marshall. "Why, that's Simon Slattery. He's a Townie. He goes to Kenton High. I know him very, very well."

"Simon Slattery? No way! That's my brother Randy's own very good friend Darryl Croft. And he goes to Foxleigh! I'm sure, because he told me so himself, and he wouldn't lie!" Jessie Brown's mouth was set in a firm, furious line.

"I'll tell you who wouldn't lie," stated Jessica Prud'homme de la Reaux. "And that's a boy from Cumberland, Taylor Windrum, cause his father knows my father."

"No," said Jody Rulolph coldly. "*I'll* tell you who

wouldn't lie. A person who respects others wouldn't lie. A person whose rommmate has been his closest friend wouldn't lie. A person who thinks of girls as people and not as puppets with strings to pull wouldn't lie. A person who can live with himself wouldn't lie. A person who doesn't play kissy-face with his reflection in a mirror wouldn't lie.''

"All *right*!'' yelled Douglas, stung to the quick. "Cut me some slack, why don't you? I was only trying to have a little fun. It was a *joke,* for God's sake . . .''

A joke! wept Joss's broken heart.

Douglas McVie took a step forward.

"Back off, slime ball!'' snarled Jody, looking mad and tough enough to take him on and beat him, two falls out of three.

"Don't come any closer. You're just lucky we're letting you live. If we wanted to, we could put you through the same humiliation that we suffered. *Plus* we could tell Grady, your housemaster, your headmaster, your parents, and all the girls at Holly Hills.''

"But you're not going to?'' Something very like a quaver of fear had crept into McVie's voice.

"No,'' said Joss icily. "And you want to know why? It's because you tried to break us apart, but you failed. You failed; we're tighter than we ever were, tighter friends than you'll ever have in your entire miserable life. We could punish you, but that would only bring us down to your level. We—we—'' she broke off, tears threatening to choke her.

"Get out!'' cried Jody furiously, protective of Joss. "Get your ass out of here and take that pretty-boy face with you. We never want to look at it again. Oh, and deliver a message to Grady for me, will you? Tell him I love him! No, never mind, I'll tell him myself!''

Without another word, Douglas turned and ran out of

the boat house. Not a moment too soon, for in the next instant Joss, crying so hard she was in danger of coming apart, threw herself into Jessie's arms and buried her face on her friend's shoulder.

"Would you like us to have a French tutorial now?" asked Jessica quickly.

"No." Joss sighed. "I'm really not up to it."

"Is there a movie on TV?" asked Jody. "We could go downstairs to the TV room."

"Nah." Jessie made a face. "Nothing we haven't seen a trillion times, just reruns of 'Gilligan's Island.' "

The Tower was sunk in gloom. It was a raw evening in mid-November, about a week before Thanksgiving break, and none of the girls seemed to have any energy. It was as though a light had gone out of them.

"Telephone," yelled somebody in the corridor. "Jessica Brown."

Jessie got up without eagerness and went to the phone. But when she came back she was smiling.

"That was Alex! He wants me to come and spend Thanksgiving with his family in Virginia."

"And are you going to?"

"Are you kidding? My mother would slam me senseless if my father didn't beat her to it. Thanksgiving is *sacred* at our house. But I did say 'yes' to Saturday night, and I invited *him* home for the Christmas holidays and he said he'd come! His parents go to Florida every year, and he's usually stuck going to his married sister's." Jessie's eyes were dancing with happiness.

In the hall, the telephone rang again.

"It's for Jessica Prooodd-whatsis!" floated up the stairs.

"Prince Charming, maybe?" kidded Jody as Jessica went down to answer it. The small girl merely blushed and shook her head, but when she returned to the Tower, her face was lit up like a Fifth Avenue store window at Christmas.

"It *was* Prince Charming! My father is coming to New York for the Thanksgiving holidays and he wants me to spend every day with him. We're staying at the Carlyle, and going to the theater, and he'll be taking me shopping by himself . . . it's going to be wonderful! And best of all, he's giving M. Leroi a ten-day vacation!"

"That's great, kid!" Jody laughed. "Make sure you buys jeans that fit."

But in a few minutes, a dull silence filled the room. Outside the windows, a gray, monotonous drizzle began to fall.

"Yo, the four Jessicas!" yelled a breathless voice. "Open the damn door!"

Jody, closest to the door, threw it open, revealing a red-faced and out-of-breath freshman, the hall monitor for the week.

"It's bad enough having to schlep up three flights of stairs without having to lug a thousand pounds of shit," grumbled the freshman, handing over her burden.

The "thousand pounds of shit" were four long white florist's boxes, tied up in red ribbons.

What the—?

There was one box for each, with a card on top. The freshman perched herself on the bed, curious to see what the four Jessicas had received. Because she'd had to carry the boxes up the stairs, she felt herself entitled, and the Jessicas were forced to agree, so they didn't push her back out in the hall.

"Everybody at once, on the count of three," ordered Jody, dodging a pillow thrown at her. "One, two—"

The ribbons came off simultaneously, to four simultaneous gasps.

Jessica Prud'homme de la Reaux pulled a large bunch of anemones and daisies and snapdragons and foxglove out of her box.

"How charming! But where on earth did he find these in November?" she breathed. She turned the white card over. The name "Taylor Windrum" was printed neatly on the card, crossed out, and the words "Douglas McVie" scrawled above it.

"The same place he found these," said Jessie, burying her nose in a fragrant bouquet of lovely lilies. Her card was like Jessica's, only the name crossed out was "Darryl Croft."

"What does your card say?" Jessica asked Jody, who was lifting a large bunch of curly-topped chrysanthemums out of their wrappings.

"It says 'Douglas McVie,' and that's crossed out and over it is written, 'Grady Ferguson's roommate and friend.' I guess they must have made up."

Only Jessica Marshall hadn't taken her floral prize from its long, white box, and the girls crowded around to see.

There was one flower in the box, only one. A perfect long-stemmed rose of the most unusual color, a blend of lavender and gray.

"Ah, the Sterling Silver rose," observed Jessica, who knew about these things. "Very rare, Joss, and *very* expensive."

But Joss only pushed the box away, her face an unreadable mask. "Take it, then. I don't want it."

The little freshman stood up. "Show's over." She yawned. "Big, fat deal, flowers. Hayfever city. Oh, yeah," she called over her shoulder as she walked out the door. "There's a boy downstairs wants to see you."

"Which one?" demanded Jody, hoping it was Grady calling on her.

"*All* of you. He's the one brought the stinkweeds. Says

his name's McVie, and he needs to talk to all of you. He signed in for the Goldfish Bowl with the four Jessicas. Isn't that a stitch? The whole dorm's buzzing.''

"Douglas McVie, *here*? What does he look like?'' Jessie asked suspiciously.

The freshman considered the question. "Kinda cute,'' she said at last, "but not as cute as Michael Jackson.'' And she vanished down the stairs like Alice down the rabbit hole.

The girls looked at one another, stunned.

"What do you think he wants?'' asked little Jessica in a whisper.

"To apologize, of course,'' said Jessie. "Just look at all these flowers. They must have set him back a couple of hundred dollars.''

"From what Grady tells me, he can afford it,'' observed Jody.

"I don't care *what* he wants, I'm not going.'' Joss shook her golden head firmly.

"I think we ought to let him grovel a little; humility is good for the soul,'' said Jody, laughing. "Besides, think what this will do for our image, the legendary lover Douglas McVie coming to beg forgiveness of the four Jessicas in the Holly Hills Goldfish Bowl in front of the whole school! It'll *make* our reputations; we'll get mileage out of that until we graduate. Maybe we can sell tickets.''

Easy for you, you didn't get your heart broken, thought Joss unhappily. You've got Grady, and Jessie has Alex, and Jessica is still a baby, and I'm the only one who got run over by a truck. Why should I forgive him? What has he done to deserve forgiveness? Spent a few bucks on flowers?

"No.'' And Joss shook her head again.

"I think it should be all of us or none of us,'' said Jessie. "We're all in this together. Let's stand together, all for

one, and one for all, like the Three Musketeers Plus One.
Remember? If Joss doesn't go downstairs, none of us do.
Okay?''

"Okay," agreed Jessica, adding unexpectedly, "it's a
shame, though. I'm perishing to hear what he could have
to say in his defense.''

"Me too," confessed Jody.

"I have to admit that I'm curious," Jessie said with New
England caution.

Joss sighed. "I can see it's three against one, instead of
all for one. Okay, I'll go. I wouldn't want to spoil your
good time, even though I'd much rather not ever see him
or speak to him again.''

"Just bear this in mind," advised Jody. "The French
have a saying: 'Revenge is a dish that people of taste prefer
to eat cold.' ''

"That's the Italians, not the French, doo-doo-head, and
you swiped that line from Amanda Cohen." This, coming
from little Jessica Prud'homme de la Reaux, made everybody laugh.

They went down together, as one, lending each other
their moral support and strength of purpose. It had
worked for them up to now.

Douglas McVie was standing at the foot of the stairs
waiting for them, and his face was a study not in arrogance
but in anxiety. When he saw them coming, a look of relief
crossed his features.

He was still perhaps the most handsome boy in the
world.

They could have met him on open ground, forced him to
say his piece in front of the eager eyes and ears of most of
the girls of Holly Hills. After all, this was a night to make
history, Douglas McVie the lady-killer eating public crow-
burger with a humble-pie chaser.

But they were intrinsically kind, and by tacit consent,

they all moved out of the main lounge to one of the smaller side rooms, for privacy. The girls took their places side by side on a sofa, staring stonily at Douglas, who perched himself on a straight-backed wooden chair. They waited in silence for him to begin.

"I realize that just saying 'I'm sorry' isn't gonna cut a helluva lot of ice with any of you," he said in a low voice with none of his usual flippancy. "But it's as good a place as any to start. Because I *am* sorry, about a lot of things, but not about everything."

"Why should we even listen to you, when every word out of your mouth so far has been one damn lie after another, and now you say you're not even sorry?" demanded Jessie. The others murmured angry assent.

"Wait, hear me out, please. For one thing, I'm not sorry that I met the four of you, and I'm really not sorry for any of the things I said to you personally. Because they were true, every word."

He turned to Jessica Brown. "Jessie, you *are* beautiful, whether you know it or not. Beautiful inside, but also beautiful outside. When I paid you compliments on your hair and eyes and figure, every word of it was true. Not only that, but you're going to become more and more beautiful the older you get. You've got that incredible bone structure. Take a took at Katharine Hepburn if you want to know what I'm talking about."

He reached over and took her hand in his very gently. "I hope I know you when you're eighty, Jessie Brown. You just might be the most beautiful woman in the world.

"As for you, Jody Rudolph, what can I say except that you're aces smarter than I am and saw right through me? And you know something? I'm glad you did. It was a stupid joke, and I'm glad it's over. I hope we can be friends, because Grady sure loves you, and I love Grady, and I want to keep his friendship and yours. And if you'll allow me to say so, he's one of the luckiest boys I ever met. Maybe even *the* luckiest.''

Turning, Douglas smiled down at little Jessica. "I gave you your first kiss and I'm glad. When you become an international beauty, I'll brag about it to everybody I meet.

"I told each and every one of you that you were unique and special. And that's no lie. Every one of you is. Not to mention that together you're as formidable an offense and defense as any team ever faced. Shit! I'm lucky I got out with my skin. The only thing I actually lost was some face and my heart. Joss . . .'' And Douglas turned, his hand held out to Jessica Marshall.

But she wasn't there. She had run out of the room, sobbing.

CHAPTER SEVENTEEN

New Initials

It rained almost all week, but on Friday the sun came out and with it came one of those surprising stretches of November weather—almost mild, with no wind. Except for Joss, who kept herself to herself, the Tower was in a great state of excitement. This was the last school weekend before the Thanksgiving break, and it was a break that everybody was looking forward to with great anticipation and excitement.

Jody Rudolph had recieved permission from her family to go home with Grady Ferguson and meet his folks. She was wearing his St. Trinity junior ring with enormous pride, on a gold chain around her neck. They were going steady, and officially engaged to be engaged to be engaged.

Jessie was dying to see her huge family again and eat her mother's cooking, but she and Alex were spending a lot of time on the telephone talking about the Christmas to come. Alex had never been as far north as Maine, and in the winter it was bound to be any ice experience for a southern boy. But Jessie was promising to keep him warm. She'd already started knitting him a sweater.

Jessica Prud'homme de la Reaux was bursting with excitement about actually spending six days with her father and no governesses or tutors or aides-de-camp to come between them. She was determined to show him how good Holly Hills had been for her, and how mature she was becoming. She even intended to leave the teddy bear back at the Tower.

Only Jessica Marshall wasn't imbued with excitement. All she had to look forward to was Moonlight Sonata, her palomino. But suddenly, she missed him enormously. On Saturday morning, when she got out of bed, the sun was shining so brightly she decided to go riding. It would be good to spend an afternoon in the saddle; it had been too long between rides. "Simon" had spoiled Joss for riding, and riding for Joss.

"It's very late in the season, Jessica," said the riding mistress. "I think it a poor idea."

"Oh, please, Mrs. Malone, it's the last possible weekend until spring! I'll be careful; I promise you that I'll not go very far, and I'll even come back in an hour if that's what you want."

"Well, all right, but only because you're an expert rider," said Mrs. Malone grudgingly, writing out the pass. "And I would like you back early. Say, two hours?"

"Oh, *thank* you, Mrs. Malone! I'll be back on time."

Mabel was waiting for her, just as though nothing had ever separated them. Whinnying, she came trotting up to Joss, who kissed her lovingly on the nose and fed her an apple from the palm of her hand.

Saddled up, Joss rode off down the trail. She had no idea what direction she'd be riding in or what trail she'd be following. The one thing she *did* know was that she wasn't going to ride within a hundred miles of the sycamore tree.

So how was it possible that Jessica Marshall found herself emerging from the woods into the meadow, riding straight for the sycamore tree? It couldn't have been her, it must have been Mabel, who knew the way so well she'd taken it automatically.

He was there, waiting by the tree, tall, broad-shouldered, and unsmiling. Beside him, Thunderbird browsed in vain for grass; it was all brown now, just stubble still damp from the rain.

Reining in, Joss turned the horse's head to take another direction. He was the last person in the world she wanted to see, or so she believed.

"Wait! Please! Joss, please wait! I need to talk to you," pleaded Douglas. "I've been waiting for two hours, just praying that you'd come."

She drew in a deep breath and squared her shoulders, but her pounding heart made a liar out of her stony exterior as she rode toward Douglas McVie.

"Jessica, please listen to me, won't you? Just give me a minute to say a few words. Only sixty seconds. You wouldn't stay long enough to listen to me the other night. Won't you hear me out today?" His face was anguished, genuinely anguished.

"I'll give you a minute and no more," she said firmly, but she didn't dare meet his eyes with her own.

"The other night I was saying that I hadn't really lied. Except for the identities. And I hadn't. I told you I love you, Joss, and I do. I never said that to any of the others, I swear. Only to you.

"The whole thing started out as a joke, but the joke turned out to be on me. Because I fell in love with you, and I was already lying through my teeth about everything else.

"Joss, sometimes I get crazy, I admit it. Maybe it's because I've always had everything I wanted, but there are times I get positively evil, and this was one of them. I *wanted* to stop, I *wanted* to tell you the truth, but I couldn't. I was already in too deep, and I was so ashamed. I guess I was punishing myself for being such a rat."

He reached out to her, and she remembered watching him stroke his horse's head so lovingly. There *was* good in him, and it had been that good she's fallen in love with. Underneath his cocky exterior was a rich vein of sweetness that had never been tapped.

"I love you, Joss, and I need you. I know I don't deserve you, but if you take my hand, maybe you can help me become a better person. If anything could do it, your love could. You were the only one of them I wanted, I swear it on the Bible, the only one I *want* out of every girl in the world. Please, Joss, give me a chance to prove that I can change. Let me show you that I can be as loyal to you as Grady is to Jody. Can't we start from the beginning, you and I?"

It was hard for Joss to speak, because doubt and hope were struggling inside her. "How could we possibly go back to the beginning again?" said Doubt.

"Be my girl, my official, formal, ring-wearing girl." Douglas smiled. "Let me show you that I can treat you like the wonderful person you are. I'll even come calling and sit in that damn Goldfish Bowl downstairs and let all of Holly Hills stare at me! Be my girl, Joss, please? Please? I'm begging you!"

His turquoise eyes looked deeply into her blue ones. She bit her lip, unable to speak, but at last she nodded yes. He grinned his delight.

"How do you do, Ms. Marshall," he said soberly, his eyes twinkling. "My name is Douglas McVie, and I'm a junior at St. Trinity. May I ride along with you?"

"Thank you. I have to be back at school in half an hour."

"By all means, then, let's hurry. I don't want my girl grounded."

They turned their horses toward the future and side by side, cantered away.

Behind them, the old sycamore tree—"their tree"—was covered with new felt initials. Now they read "J.M." and "D. McV."

It must have taken him hours.

Just wait until she told the other Jessicas.

About the Author

Leonore Fleischer is the author of AGNES OF GOD, BENJI, ICE CASTLES, ANNIE, FAME, STAYING ALIVE, HEAVEN CAN WAIT, A STAR IS BORN and THE ROSE. She lives in New York with her son and cat. The cat has four other cats.